Sleuths
and
Truths

*∴*Girl*∴*Writer*∴*

Sleuths and Truths

Ros Asquith

PICCADILLY PRESS • LONDON

For Jessie, with love

First published in Great Britain in 2007
by Piccadilly Press Ltd.,
5 Castle Road, London NW1 8PR
www.piccadillypress.co.uk

A catalogue record for this book is available
from the British Library

ISBN: 978 1 85340 910 3

1 3 5 7 9 10 8 6 4 2

Printed and bound in Great Britain by Bookmarque Ltd
Typeset by M Rules, London
Cover illustration by Bernice Lum
Cover design by Simon Davis

Set in 11.25 point Novarese Book and 10 point Comic Sans

Chapter One

Laura Hunt's Top Tips for Budding Writers:
Find a quiet place to write that feels as
if it's special to you. It can be anywhere as
long as it makes you feel comfortable.

*I tried writing in bed and two things happened. I fell asleep
and Xerxes ate a whole chapter. Do other cats eat paper?
Does he need to go to the vet? Or a psychiatrist?*

I am writing this in a tree.

I'm waiting for Callum.

I'm furious with Viola.

I only wanted to help her out, because I'd heard her dad
was in prison. And now she just doesn't want to know me.

Sorry, Dear Reader, are you lost?

I get carried away with writing sometimes. My Aunt Laura,
who's a proper writer, is always telling me I shouldn't take for
granted that readers know what I'm talking about just
because it makes sense to me.

So you might be asking: Who's Callum? Who's Viola?

Who's her dad? Why is he in prison? And why a tree?

This is the tree house in my best friend Callum's garden. His dad built it for Callum when he was six. Callum, that is, not his dad. It's not one of those tree houses you see in posh catalogues, all made like cabins with rope ladders and bunks and tellies and stuff, looking like something out of *Hello!* magazine. It's just rough old planks knocked together with some windows and a roof that Callum's dad got from a broken garden shed, but it's quite cosy – you can keep dry up here if the rain is falling straight down, but not if it's slanty. There's even a shelf with a toy horse of mine on it, and some ancient model cars.

Callum and I brought a treasure chest up here when we were nine and filled it with emergency rations and old teddies and an atlas and a compass, in case we ever needed to run away. We used to spend every Saturday up here in the clouds until last spring term, when we decided to give up the tree house because we had to grow up and go to secondary school. Some bloke in the Bible said a time comes when you have to 'put away childish things'. But now it's the Christmas holidays and we are both grown-up enough to realise that childhood shouldn't be thrown away lightly, and that playing in tree houses is what everybody wants to do all their lives really, but they either:

a) get too old and creaky and stiff, or
b) feel stupid sitting in a tree when they could be doing something useful like planning their next

kitchen conversion, or complaining about why they can't park anywhere these days or why teenagers' jeans hang down – you know the sort of thing adults are always going on about.

So now we're reunited with the tree. We've had some great times up here. We cooked sausages on a little camping stove once, until it fell over and nearly burned the place down, so after that we sadly had to admit that tree-cooking was a bad idea. We've written songs up here, played Monopoly (we made a space on the board for the tree house, in place of Marylebone Station, which we'd never heard of), we might even have played Doctors and Nurses up among the twigs, but I don't want to go into THAT.

Oh, I haven't told you about Viola, have I? She's my other best friend, at Falmer North School. Or at least, she WAS. She's been avoiding me all holidays and it's making me mad and sad. But more sad.

It is cold in the tree, because it is December 29th and it has been snowing for two days despite global warming, and I am muffled up with three scarves, four pairs of socks and a stripy glove. I would be wearing two stripy gloves, but my lazy old flea-bitten cat Xerxes has stolen one and is keeping it for his pet. I am wondering if this means Xerxes is lonely.

I am certain my goldfish, Blue, is lonely. My Aunt Laura says that's why she has two cats, although I think it's a bit mean of her to call them both Joan. You would think a writer would have more imagination. I asked for a friend for Blue for Christmas, and Candice – that's my mum – got me a little goldfish castle and some weed. I have put the weed and the castle in Blue's tank, but he doesn't seem to have cheered up. I think it is because he needs the company of a real live warm-blooded friend, like we all do. Howard – that's my dad – gave me a book token with a picture of a tropical fish on it which I have propped beside Blue's tank, but he doesn't pay it much attention.

I am going to get out of this tree in exactly two minutes unless Callum comes up here.

'CALLUM! YOU HAVE ONE MINUTE, FIFTY-FIVE SECONDS OR ELSE I AM GOING HOME.'

Well, that is what I roared from the top of our tree house, just as I have roared it most weekends since we were six. I had to roar it eight more times and by then I was ten minutes older and two hours colder, but he did come eventually, clambering up the old rope ladder, muffled up inside what looked like a dead sheep.

'Why are you wearing a dead sheep?'

'Don't you like it?' From what I could see of his face, he looked quite upset. 'Mum knitted it for me for Christmas.'

'Sorry, well, I only meant . . . well, all jumpers look like dead sheep don't they? I mean, you know, wool . . .'

'They don't have to *kill* sheep to make jumpers, do they?' came the muffled but scornful voice of Callum. 'Think of the number of woolly jumpers there are, not to mention socks and scarves and hats for hippies. There wouldn't be any sheep left. They give the sheep a haircut, or woolcut, and then it grows some more.'

Callum had gone a strange purple colour while he was making this speech, as if he were being strangled. In fact, he looked as if he were being strangled by a dead sheep.

'Callum, what's the matter? Have you got foot-and-mouth disease?'

'My mum made this especially for me. And now you're saying it doesn't suit me!' he choked.

'All right, it's great, it's lovely!' I yelled, half frightened and half cross.

'Hah!' He pulled the thing off, roaring with laughter and dangled it above his head, before throwing it out of the tree-house. It was indeed a dead sheep. Or at least, it was an old sheepskin. It didn't have a head or legs or anything.

'Callum, that's disgusting!'

'Sorry,' he managed to gulp. 'I had a bet with Mum that I could make you say it suited me. It's an old fleece I used to lie on when I was a baby.'

I hit him on the head with this very diary.

'I've been sitting up here freezing, waiting for you to come and help me with my great work, and all you do is dress up as a dead sheep.'

'It was warm, though,' said Callum through chattering teeth.

'Can I borrow your scarf?'

'Which one?'

We huddled under my coat for a bit.

'What's the point of anything if you don't have love in your life?' I said after a long pause.

'You've got me,' Callum said, showing how much he meant it by pulling my coat off me and on to him. I tugged it back again and he groaned.

'I was thinking Blue needed a warm-blooded friend to make him happy.'

'Who's Blue?' Callum asked, yawning.

'Fish. You know that.'

'You mean a cold-blooded friend, then.'

I considered this.

'True. I wonder if in fish literature they would say "my blood runs warm" when they're frightened? Or whether "she has a heart of ice" would be, like, an enormous compliment?'

'Exactically,' Callum said.

I think brilliant authors, like I am going to be, need to know things like this. How can you get into a character's mind and heart unless you can imagine who they really are? And that should even include fish, shouldn't it? I must ask Aunt Laura, who is Queen of children's fiction, about this.

'But I do mean me, too, not just Blue,' I said to Callum.

'Expand, using examples,' Callum said in a deep, teacherly voice. I think his posh new school, Arlington Oratory, is getting to him. It seems to think that kids even have to spend all the Christmas holidays up to their armpits in Latin verbs. Since Callum is dyslexic in English, I cannot see how he is supposed to spell in Latin, but with the money his parents are paying for him to go there, anything's possible.

'Well, I wanted to be writing the first chapters of my fantastic new Victorian detective adventure series, but I can't concentrate because I KEEP thinking about my friend Viola. She's avoiding me.'

'Is it anything you said? Have you told her she smells? Or her father used to be a woman, or something like that?' Callum asked.

'I haven't said anything to her. I haven't had the chance. It's such a shame, because the heroine of my detective story is a bit like Viola actually. She's very clever but very shy. She is going to be called Shirley Holmes and she is the younger sister of the extremely famous sleuth, Sherlock Holmes. She's twice as clever as her brother, but her thrilling exploits have been concealed for decades by jealous pipe-smoking men, in an attempt to avoid humiliation. It will be I, Cordelia Arbuthnott, who reveals her brilliant detective work, which has lain undiscovered all these years!'

'That explains why she's avoiding you,' Callum groaned, pulling the coat over again. 'You've gone nuts.'

'No, no, I'm sure this book will make my name, if I can only get it written. But I have to find out the real secret of Viola's silence, that's the key to carrying on with it.'

There was a bit of a distraction at this point, because Xerxes, who often follows me all the way to Callum's house (because he gets pampered rotten by Callum's cat-loving mum) turned up to have his regular argument with Callum's cat, Einstein. Callum called him that, for some reason to do with physics – I think the cat's mass times its acceleration squared equals nought, or something, which would make sense as this cat does even more lying around than Xerxes.

'Go away, Xerxes,' I snapped at him. 'This is a private conversation.'

Xerxes, standing in the tree-house doorway with his back arched, just snarled. Einstein was on the window ledge, snarling back.

'They're having their own private conversation,' Callum said, after this snarling business had gone on for a bit.

Then Xerxes did something I don't think I'd ever seen him do before – he sprang across the tree house at Einstein, so Callum and I had to fling ourselves out of the way, and with a furious yelp, Einstein disappeared from the window ledge.

'Cor,' said Callum, peering out of the door. 'He's out there just hanging on by his claws. Hold my legs.'

I had to grab hold of Callum round his knobbly knees while he leaned out to try to catch Einstein. Xerxes sat triumphantly on the window ledge wagging his tail, and I'm sure he was smiling.

'This is all your fault, Xerxes,' I groaned, panting. 'You're a troublemaker.'

'I think I've got him,' came the distant voice of Callum. 'OWWWW!!'

'What's happening?' I said, panicking.

'I've dropped him!' Callum screeched.

I hauled myself over Callum and stuck my head out of the door just in time to see Einstein perform a graceful somersault in the air and land in the snow-covered com-post heap the right way up. He shook the snow off each paw in turn very carefully, and delicately picked his way out of the compost heap, giving us an amazingly cool look before slinking off.

'That's the last time I do him a favour,' Callum said, nursing the scratch on his hand. 'Amazing landing, though. He looked like James Bond after he's just crashed a tank through a wall and fought twenty-five mad ninjas. You know, straightening his tie as if nothing had happened.'

Obviously disappointed by Einstein's escape, Xerxes tried the consolation prize of burrowing into the coat for a kip, but we shooed him out.

'Don't come back unless you've got my other glove,' I said to his disappearing rear end.

'Anyway,' Callum said, 'what's this new Big Idea for a book?'

I took a deep breath.

'Well, Shirley Holmes is a brilliant detective, much better than her brother, and she's going to solve a bigger mystery than anything he has ever solved. Also, I thought I might combine a good Victorian name from another book, so it will grab readers who like romance as well as detective stories: it's called The Bat of the D'Urbervilles – what do you think?'

I stopped, puffing hard.

Callum looked thoughtful. His ears, which were going blue with the cold, started flapping, which they always do when he worries about something. My heart sank. Callum is my biggest fan so if he didn't like the idea, then I must be on the wrong track.

'You don't like it,' I moaned. 'I have already spent two whole days working on this idea. I have thought of nothing else since Boxing Day, and you don't like it. Why? What's wrong with it?'

'It's not that I don't like it,' he said carefully. 'It's just that, I can't believe that no one's had that idea already. Shirley Holmes. It's a bit, well, obvious, isn't it? I bet some loony feminist's already done it.'

'Obvious? I thought it was really clever! And feminists aren't loony. They're right!' I could feel a nasty lump rising in my throat.

'No, it IS clever. It's a great idea, really. It's just the name, Shirley, you know . . .' he trailed off, seeing I was close to tears. 'You're upset about something else, aren't you?'

'No, I'm not upset about anything,' I said, huffily. 'Why would I be upset about sitting up here freezing while you're hours late, and then you make an idiot of me with your sheep thing and then you hate my book just because you're getting clever with Latin and stuff, and no one gives me any help with my writing. Nobody cares about it!'

'What about Viola? I thought she loved your writing.'

'I told you,' I wailed. 'She doesn't want to know me any more.' And then it all came tumbling out.

I told Callum that, although I have had Viola over to my house about ten times since we made friends last term, she has never, not even once, asked me back to her house. I told him about how my last story *The Lady of the Rings*, which I had thought was a fabulous romance, had won the comedy prize at school because Viola had entered it in the comedy section.

'I know she did that, but that was to help you, wasn't it?'

'Yes, yes, it was,' I admitted. 'But since then she just seems to have been avoiding me. And, well, I've been wondering if what Tobylerone said about her is true . . .'

'Tobylerone? You mean that huge boy with the triangular head? What did he say?'

'He said that Viola was probably like the rest of her family. Dishonest . . .'

'What do you mean?'

'He said her dad was in prison. And I think he might have told Viola that he told me. And that's maybe why she's avoiding me.'

'Aha,' said Callum. 'Has she ever talked about her dad to you?'

'She changes the subject. She did say he was away a lot.'

'Well, if it's true then she might be ashamed of you knowing. But if her dad's in prison, it's not her fault. It's not a reason to be mean to her.'

'I'm NOT being mean to her. She's being mean to ME. She never asks me home! I haven't heard from her all Christmas holidays! She didn't even send me a Christmas card! I spent ages making her a card,' I said pathetically. 'It's difficult for me, because I am not good at drawing like you are.' (Callum is the most brilliant artist I have ever met. I think he is going to be a great painter one day, as long as the boring old Arlington Oratory school lets him be creative and doesn't stuff his head so full of Latin and physics that he forgets how to draw, which is what happens to most kids when they hit twelve and forget how to have fun.)

'And I wrote a whole lot of stuff in the card about what a great friend she'd been and how she'd made disgusting old Falmer North seem like a nice school, and how much I looked forward to next term because of her, and how I hoped we'd meet up in the holidays, and how I was looking forward to meeting her folks, which I suppose was a bit of a hint . . .' I trailed off.

'What do you mean, hint?' asked Callum.

'Well, like, trying to get her to ask me round.'

'Well, if it's true about her dad, maybe she's shy about you coming round because you might start wondering why he isn't there. And there might be all criminals' stuff lying around: crowbars and pump-action shotguns, and stocking masks and signed photos of murderers.'

I sighed. 'That's not very likely, is it?'

'Have you texted her?'

'Three times. Nothing back.'

'Your battery's usually dead,' Callum said.

He has a point, though I didn't like to admit it.

'I checked it last night. The only message was from you.'

In fact, Callum is the only person who ever calls my

mobile, which is probably why I haven't bothered with it much since my two best friends from primary school moved away. I am not exactly the world's most wanted person socially, which may be because I call my parents Howard and Candice, or may be because I like sitting in trees and wearing green velvet dresses and writing books. But I am not going to change all that just to be popular.

'It's just, I thought Viola was different. I thought she understood me, you know, like you do.'

Callum was silent for a bit. His ears, now purple, flapped gently. I could see he was thinking very hard.

'We need a plan,' he said. 'Remember that silly rhyme we used to sing up here? Whenever we needed help with something?'

'Yes,' I said mournfully. 'But that was easy stuff like putting a spell on Miss Tarbuck, or getting days off school, or persuading your dad to let us get a McDonalds . . .'

'How did it go?' asked Callum.

I knew he knew and was only trying to buck me up, but we both put our hands on the trunk of the tree and I began:

> One, two, tree
> Please do this thing for me
> Show me a way
> Show me today
> To shake off this curse and be FREE!

We banged our hands on the tree trunk.

'But it isn't really a curse,' I said. 'It's just not knowing whether Viola's dad's in prison or not.'

'We could have had a curse about dungeons and things,' said Callum, rather regretfully. 'Anyway, it's given me an idea. We'll search for his name on the internet and see if it tells us where he is.'

'You think the internet knows about everything,' I said, annoyed. 'You're so like a boy.'

Callum wriggled about a bit and peeked down inside his jeans.

'Phew. That's a relief. I was still a boy last time I looked, but that was seconds ago. Should I check again?'

'Idiot.'

'Poltroon.'

'I'm not writing poltroon or olden dayes of yore stuff any more, I'm writing Victorian detective melodrama.'

'Then let's look up some Victorian melodrama insults on the internet and try Viola's dad at the same time. It just might work, and we had better do it before our fingers fall off with frostbite and ruin the careers of a budding novelist and a young artist cut down in his prime.'

We retreated to the warmth of Callum's room. Of course, we tried hard, but what did we have to go on?

'You mean you don't even know his name?' Callum was getting annoyed.

'Well, Viola's surname is Larpent, but I know that Toby-lerone called him something else, I just can't remember what it was . . . something like Dizzy Stokes, like a nickname . . .'

We tried Googling 'Larpent' and 'jail' and 'prison' and 'robbery' and 'criminal'. But all we got was ancient war heroes and Her Majesty's Prison reports.

The internet can be a very soulless thing. We cheered ourselves up, though, by finding some Victorian slang for my book.

'Hoysting haybag!' shouted Callum.

'Don't you dare call me a shoplifting woman, you glocky gonoph!' I replied, quick as a flash, my wits glinting in the glow of Callum's state-of-the-art computer.

Callum's house is full of posh gadgets because Peter and Andrea, his folks, are both therapists who get paid millions, according to my folks, for just sitting there listening to people moan on about their problems.

'As long as people are miserable,' says Howard, 'Peter and Andrea will never be out of work. Like undertakers.'

'Glocky gonoph?' said Callum, wrenching me back to Victorian reality.

'It means half-witted, small-time criminal, apparently. I hope that's what Viola's dad is, if he's anything at all,' I said. 'I hope he's not . . .' my voice trailed off. Callum knew I was thinking of terrible things, but neither of us wanted to Google 'Larpent' with 'murder' or something, at least, not in front of each other, so I changed the subject and rabbitted on about words.

'What happens to these words? Look at this: "kenet-seeno kanurd"! It means stinking drunk! Why do they just die out? It's sad to think words are an endangered species, or dead already, like dodos . . .'

'Yeah. But YOU are going to bring them back to life with your amazing book!' said Callum encouragingly.

'And YOU can bring them back to life with your amazing pictures,' I said. 'Your first task is to draw a haybag wearing luggers and carrying . . . oh look, look at this fantastic old word for umbrella – bumbershoot.'

'You'll need a bumbershoot to get home,' said Callum. I looked out to see that the light snowfall had turned into a a blizzard.

I had that sad feeling you get when Christmas is over and it hasn't been quite like you had hoped it would be. This was the first snowy year that Callum and I had not taken advantage of it and gone sledging or built a snowman. We had always longed for snow when we were younger, and now we had it and we hadn't played in it at all. I suddenly understood what Howard had said once, about grown-ups wanting to have kids. It's so they can do those things again without feeling they're too old and stupid to do them. It's like with the tree house.

'Let's have a snowball fight,' said Callum, reading my thoughts as only he can do.

We ran out on to Callum's snowy lawn, and hurtled off in different directions to take cover behind bushes. We were both a bit out of practice – it doesn't snow that often. My first snowball hit Callum's kitchen window with a loud thump, and the cleaner, Anastasia, came out of the back door, shouting at us in Polish or Russian or something. We both turned on her at once, my snowball flying into the kitchen and setting off an indignant howl from the invisible Einstein, Callum's hitting the door and splattering over Anastasia. Unexpectedly, she sprang into the garden, scooped up a snowball, and hit Callum in the ear while he was still standing up to admire his handiwork. Then she ran back in, chortling, and slammed the door.

Callum and I chased each other out of the side gate into the street. I got him with a good one just before he made it to a wheelie bin, and he caught me on the bum as I was bending down to reload. Then I ran towards the bin yelling, a snowball in each hand. Callum, who'd been stocking up, let loose three in quick succession. They all whistled past me, but then I heard a deep voice saying:

'Assaulting an officer in the execution of his duty, eh?'

I looked round in horror to see a large policeman behind me, his dark uniform splattered with snow.

'Ohmigod, I'm sorry, we were just . . .'

The policeman bent down in a dignified way, scooped up some snow and hit Callum, who was just emerging from behind the bin, very accurately in the middle of his chest. Callum didn't know whether to look apologetic or laugh.

'I'm PC Budakli,' he said. 'I'm your community copper. Where do you go to school?'

I told him. But Callum just mumbled. 'Falmer North, eh?' he said. 'I'm going to be manning the crossing outside there soon. I expect I'll see you again. Watch the snowballs. You might hit a car, and the driver won't be as understanding as me.'

He started to walk off, with that slow step policemen on the beat have.

'Aren't you going to arrest us, or anything?' Callum asked. He sounded as if he quite fancied the idea.

'First offence,' PC Budakli said, smiling. 'Let you off this time. Next time, of course, I'll put you in chains.'

'He was nice, wasn't he?' I said to Callum, as we headed round the corner to my house.

'Yeah,' Callum said. 'Good shot, too. Must be the training. But he was nothing on Anastasia. She must have been trained in the Special Forces, Cleaning Division.'

We got to my gate.

'When you're back at school we can just follow Viola home,' Callum said. 'Maybe that way we'll find out what she's trying to hide.'

'Doesn't seem right,' I said, 'spying on a mate. She's probably just gone off me.'

I realised, as I waved goodbye to Callum and then promptly tripped over Xerxes in the hall, that Viola was the first new friend I'd had in ages, and I didn't want to let her go. I gave Blue a pinch of fish food and promised myself I would buy a friend for him this very week. And maybe a change of diet might cheer him up. I wondered if all those different coloured flakes actually tasted different.

Over supper I tried to talk to Candice about Viola,

although of course I didn't mention the stuff about her dad being in prison. It would scare her.

'I'm sure you'll make lots of new friends next term,' was all she said. Then she added, 'Viola's a sweet girl of course, but . . .'

'But what?'

'Well, she's very quiet, isn't she? She doesn't really seem to be your sort of person. What do her parents do?'

'Oh, her dad's a surgeon,' I lied. 'And her mum's a playwright. Think she's got something coming out in the West End soon.'

'Really?' said Candice, brightening. 'Well, of course you must ask her to tea again the minute you get back. I expect they're off on some last-minute skiing trip and that's why you haven't heard from her.'

Suddenly, this seemed like an Aunt Laura moment. Aunt Laura and I have always been really close, because she is a writer. I really needed advice, so I emailed her, telling her the whole story and begging her not to mention a word to Candice. This is what she emailed back:

```
Darling Cordy,
How lovely to hear from you but I am so
sorry you are DID. (That's Aunt Laura's
shorthand for Down in the Dumps.)
    I think it's probably better not to
try to dig too deep into Viola's life
just now. It may be that she doesn't
```

want you to know. If she did, you must
realise she would tell you. There may be
some perfectly good reason why she has
not been in touch over Christmas and the
thing about her father sounds a little
as though it could just be an ugly
rumour. But even if it's true, remember,
this isn't one of your stories, it's
real life. If your friend wants to keep
something private, it's her choice. I
think the best thing you can do is be
really friendly to her when term begins
and not to snoop about too much! If you
snoop, you're bound to put her off!! And
I'm sure Candice is right and that you
will make new friends at Falmer North
next term. You are too young to put
AYEIOB!! (This is short for All Your Eggs In One
Basket. This habit of Aunt Laura's and all her
annoying exclamation marks are two of the reasons
that Candice thinks she is a not very good writer.)
But I'm absolutely DELIGHTED to hear
about your Victorian melodrama detective
story. I hope there will be plenty of
thrills and spills and perhaps a murder
or two, although nothing tooo gory!
Can't wait to see it!!

    Joan and Joan loved the catnip cake

you sent them. I hope Xerxes wasn't too
jealous but I am sure you baked one for
him too. I must say it travelled very
well, even though it got a bit squished
by the poor postie trying to shove it
through the letterbox. I'm afraid the
Three Bees (these are Bessie, Bobby and Bertie,
Aunt Laura's mad triplet grandchildren, who have so
far been rushed to hospital six times for eating
worms, loo cleaner etc, and they are only three)
had quite a lot of it and were very
sick, but *c'est la vie*.

OOOODLES of love darling and do
please send me instalments of *The Bride
of Dracula*!!!

Your devoted Auntie Lolly

PS I didn't want to say this sweetie,
but I'm afraid the name Shirley Holmes
HAS been used already. There was a TV
series of that name way back before the
dinosaurs in the 1990s. And I fear
there were a few spin-off books as
well. I'm sure they were nothing like
as good as your own will be, however.
But perhaps you should change your
heroine's name? Sheila? Shelley? Or you
could have a fab BOY detective like
Alex Rider. LOOK how successful those

```
books are!! Makes me quite jealous,
although of course that sort of book is
not really my THING!!
```

Great. Aunt Laura has not exactly fulfilled my wildest hopes and dreams. She hates my idea of spying on Viola and she has blown my great book idea. Why did she have to tell me there was already a Shirley Holmes? And a *boy* detective! Doesn't she realise I am a feminist? Anyway, Alex Rider is a James Bond figure, which is totally different. I wonder if Aunt Laura is getting a bit out of touch?

Oh well. I'm wrong about that. I see from her website that her latest book, A *Time To Weep* is top of the charts again and has an even pinker sparklier cover than usual. She has these amazing girly covers with sequins on, but all her stories are about 'issues' like divorce and bed-wetting and stuff. I want to write about adventure, and mystery, and romance. But you've got to hand it to Aunt Laura, she's the girls' fiction Queen.

I looked at her email again. 'Oooodles of love.' 'Can't wait to see it.' She is, surely, the best aunt anyone ever had. Perhaps I should admit that she's my aunt at school. So far only Viola knows. Maybe it would be a way of making other friends . . .

New Year's Day.

Callum has flu. Candice has flu. Howard and I tried to see
the New Year in with her, but she was snoring softly when we
got into the bedroom and we didn't have the heart to wake
her up.

'Whisky and hot lemon,' Howard said. 'It's a great home
cure. Not if you want to stay up late, though.'

'Let's go and turn the telly on,' I said, taking his arm. 'We
can listen to Big Ben and sing "Auld Lang Syne", whatever
that means.'

The central heating had gone off, so we sat up wrapped
in an old blanket and toasted the New Year with warm beer
as he had forgotten to get any champagne.

'Happy New Year, Dad,' I said, hugging him. He's all
right, my dad. Cuddly, like a teddy, but with the brains of

a professor. Which, of course, he is. 'What will it bring?'

'Bills,' he said.

'What kind of attitude is that?' I asked him. 'I know you don't get paid a quarter of what you should, but this is a time of optimism and hope. All over the world people are saying things are going to get better.'

'Mugs,' said Howard.

I punched him in the ribs.

'Ow,' he grumbled. 'But you're right. I'm a grumpy old git. Time for new plans, grand schemes, the great leap forward!'

This Big Moment for Howard didn't last long because Aunt Laura, who annoys him, rang up. He exchanged greetings with her pretty briefly and handed the phone to me.

'Cordy! Happy New Year, darling! Hope you're not too DID with everyone having the flu! The Three Bees have all woken up for a ghastly midnight feast and are longing to say Happy New Year!'

First Bee: 'Hubby new ear.'

Second Bee: 'Hippy new beer.'

Third Bee: Horrible choking noise and phone goes dead.

'What happened?' Howard asked. He looked more than ever like a giant teddy bear in his old-fashioned dressing gown and stripy pyjamas.

'I think one of the triplets just died,' I told him anxiously. Alarmed teddy bear phoned Laura back.

'All OK. Bee Three just swallowed a cork. Apparently Laura smacked it on its back and the cork popped out just like a bottle of bubbly.'

Great. At least a cork is popping somewhere in this weary world . . .

Am now curled up in bed with Xerxes on my head. He thinks I am his basket. I have tried saying, 'I am not a basket. I am a person.' But Xerxes does not know the difference.

I should have some New Year's Resolutions. Here they are:

1) School in two days – ignore Viola and concentrate on My Art.
2) Have my name embossed in silver, or maybe gold, on a whole row of books in every bookshop in the land.
3) Write so many books, nobody in the world can fail to know about me.

You might have read that old Enid Blyton, who wrote not just *Noddy* but also the *Famous Five* and *The Secret Seven*, wrote one book a WEEK for a whole YEAR. So that is fifty-two books in one year. That makes even the fabulous and brilliant Jacqueline Wilson look a bit slow, doesn't it? And JK Rowling has been taking a whole two years . . . But of course, I will write great works of literature, whether it takes me ten weeks or ten years, because I am determined! And to anyone who says my lifelong ambition isn't very long yet, seeing as how I am not quite twelve, I just say, erm, 'poo'. Which may not be very authorly of me, but it's the best I can think of right now.

Alliteration is my big thing at the moment. That's when you write a sentence using lots of words that start with the same letter, to enhance the atmosphere. Like 'softly swishing sea' or 'swiftly swooping seagull'. You'll see lots of alliteration in my fab new detective story I'm writing: *The Bat of the D'Urbervilles*. I have actually written quite a lot of it already, so I'll share it with you, Dear Reader, as no one else will probably ever read it.

The Bat of the D'Urbervilles

Charlotte Holmes paced her shadowy, spooky, smoky booklined study.

She coughed.

'Curses!' she spluttered, Victorianly. 'If I had the money of my brother, Sherlock, I could afford to send small boys up to clean the chimneys, and live in a big beautiful apartment like 221B Baker Street. However, the asthmatic atmosphere in here may have the same effect as his horrible pipe-smoking, and concentrate my mind on the problems at hand.'

On she paced, pondering the perplexing puzzle of problems the day's papers had presented, her Stradivarius violin perched precariously upon her shoulder, like a peregrine pursuing its prey, furrowed deep in thought, wrestling with an insuperably convoluted conundrum. What could be the meaning of the ailing infants of Aylesbury? Who was behind the dastardly disappearance of demure damsels in Dunbar? And the beastly burglary from the

Barnstaple blood bank? Could the three bizarre events be connected?

Just as Holmes was pondering these problems, her faithful apprentice, Dr Callum Watson, burst in, his hair akimbo, his arms awry. His glasses, which usually perched peacefully on his snubby, snouty nose, were now steamy with distress.

'We have a visitor, Holmes, and he is in a state of high anxiety.' Watson had hardly spoken these words when, sure enough, just as he had predicted, a cadaverous character in his mid-forties with long fine flowing fair hair and a dark brow furrowed with fury – or was it fear? – strode swiftly into the study in Watson's wake.

'High anxiety indeed, Watson,' Holmes murmured with a slight sarcastic smirky smile. 'Our guest must be six foot four if he's an inch.'

'A very palpable perspicacious point, Holmes,' Watson said admiringly. 'Your rapier-like wit knows no bounds.'

Holmes hovered, her sharp, pointed ears alert for the slightest hint of a clue as to where this preposterous person had come from. Then she suddenly spun, quickly casting her bright, beady blue eyes in the stranger's direction.

In an instant, her supple sight, knowledgeable nostrils and effective ears had summed the intruder up.

'I see you have consumed a roulade in Romania, a korma in Kurdistan, a marshmallow in Milton Keynes and a bagel in Birmingham,' she said, to the astonished stranger, who stopped, astonished, as Holmes continued without pausing for breath. 'Yet your mother, I fancy, was from Transylvania. What interests me, though, is how things were when you took vodka and vermouth with the Viscount of Vladivostok at Waterloo last Wednesday?'

'How does she do it?' thought Dr Callum Watson, his simple face alight with admiration.

Holmes paused to gaze thoughtfully at her fingernails, glazed with a dusting of palest pink pearlised polish, which was one of her few submissions to the frightful femininity thrust upon women of her historical period. She paused to wait while the full brilliance of her assessment dawned upon the visitor.

But the astonished visitor had recovered himself. Flicking up his tailcoat he seated himself squarely in the single vacant chair opposite Holmes's desk and fixed her with his luminous glassy eyes.

'It was the Viscount of Verona, as it happens,' he said.

Holmes allowed the corner of her lip to curl into a thin smile. Here was someone she could do business with.

'And how may I help?' she enquired.

And so it was that Sir Horatio D'Urberville, the fourteenth Earl of D'Urberville, recently returned from abroad to take up residence in D'Urberville Hall, the ancient stately home of his D'Urberville forefathers, who had resided there for thirteen generations in the lap of luxury, began to reveal to Holmes and Watson his blood-curdling story. The tale he unravelled as twilight fell in the Baker Street basement, was, in actual fact, so blood-curdling that it even curdled the blood of Holmes and Watson, those most uncurdled of dauntless detectives.

'There is a curse upon us!' cried Sir Horatio D'Urberville, holding aloft his frayed, fluttering hands in front of his twitching, tremulous face.

And out poured his gruesome story.

Laura Hunt's Top Tips for Budding Writers:
Make absolutely sure you have an exciting beginning (and an exciting middle and an exciting end!).

This is a tall order. How about: 'THE END OF THE WORLD WAS NIGH. CHARLOTTE HOLMES ALONE COULD SAVE IT'. Or should I just pretend I am falling out of the tree?

Chapter Two

Flapping about in my room, trying to get cat hair off something vaguely nice to wear. V. nervous about first day back at school.

How am I going to ignore Viola? Walk past her with my nose in the air? Turn my back on her?

It would be so much easier if I had another friend, but I haven't really got to know anyone properly. There's the dreaded Jolene and Zandra, who we know as the banshees, and there's the supermodel lookalike, Buff Barbara. I got to know her when we thought Callum's dad had got a girlfriend (which you can read all about in my first amazing book) but she's in Year Eleven. She's very nice and everything, and going around with her makes you feel you might have your pic in a fashion magazine any minute – but I can't see her telling her almost-as-cool-looking friends to get lost so she can hang around with me.

I shouldn't have put all my eggs in one basket as Aunt Laura so kindly said. I should have spread myself thinner. But Viola and I were so close last term. She wants to be a writer as badly as I do and I thought she was the girl friend I'd been waiting for all my life.

'CORDELIA!!!!!'

That's my mother, trying to make our house fall down with shouting, as usual. If you can get arrested for disturbing the peace, I don't know why the police aren't round here every day. I'm surprised she isn't more worried about her precious ceramic objects just falling to bits with the shock.

Ever since she opened her gallery, the house has got more and more stuffed with arty pottery – you can hardly walk up the stairs without bashing into a pyramid of teapots shaped like shoehorns or bumbershoots. Or else ashtrays in the shape of canoes. I said to her, 'Why are you selling ashtrays? Nobody's allowed to smoke any more, except at school.'

Of course, this brought out her insane worry-mode.

'Darling, they don't smoke in *class* do they? In year SEVEN? Surely not?'

It is very easy to wind Candice up, because she doesn't really think I should be with the hoodies and banshees of Falmer North, but in a nice posh school like Callum's, wearing a navy blazer and a pleated skirt like she used to.

She probably thinks even the teachers are drug-dealers at Falmer North. But she and Howard can't afford school fees, so we're stuck with it.

I wish I knew what I thought about all that stuff. There are people at Falmer North I know I never would have met at a school like Callum's – well, I haven't met most of them, but Aunt Laura's always telling me that lots of different experiences are like food and drink to a writer, and they don't come much more different than people like Tobylerone and the banshees. I try to imagine them in Victorian clothes so I can put them in my book, and Aunt Laura's right, it's a big help. Sometimes just thinking those thoughts makes me smile.

On the other hand, I quite like pleated skirts and navy blazers, and maybe at a school like that I wouldn't feel so weird and different for not wearing a belly stud and sending stupid texts all day to people in the next room.

Sigh. It's not easy being an Artist. Maybe I'll just have to make *The Bat of the D'Urbervilles* into a hot bestseller so we can afford the school fees.

'CORDELIA!!!'

There she goes again.

Aaargh. It's Viola on the phone. Candice has already told her I'm on my way down.

I picked up the receiver.

'I'm feeling nervous about school. Can I walk in with you?' was all Viola said.

What a cheek.

'I'm walking in with Buff Barbara,' I said wildly.

Silence. Then the little, miserable, tearful, vole-like voice of Viola said, 'Oh.'

Normally this would have tugged at my heartstrings, but I remained firm.

'See you later,' I said. And put the phone down!

Candice was eavesdropping, as usual. 'Why did you say that? I thought you liked Viola?'

'Tell you later,' I snarled, grabbing my school bag. I wanted to give her a hug and tell her all about it, but I couldn't stand the agonised look of worry that besmirches her mug whenever I'm upset. She always gets so anxious that you'd think it was HER who had the problem. It's not very comforting.

I ignored Viola all day, which meant I didn't speak to anyone much. It was miserable. The only good bit was our cuddly, kind form tutor Mrs Warren – whose ears I swear have grown upwards and her teeth downwards in the holidays, so she looks even more like a rabbit than usual – being all kind and friendly and pleased to see us.

I wished I could hide behind my hair like Viola did when PC Budakli came in. Luckily, he didn't make any snowball jokes, just introduced himself and said he'd be 'popping in and out' to give us tips on how to avoid muggings etc. By the look of some of the Year Tens, he should be telling them how to avoid *doing* muggings, but I was hoping to corner him later for a few tips to help me with my best-selling, world-record-beating detective series.

Otherwise, I was moping about trying to avoid Viola all day until it got to English, when of course Mrs Parsing would be bound to make me and Viola sit together, because she thinks we are her 'young hopeful' writers.

'I want you all to get into pairs and find yourselves a nosey little cook in the library,' she winked. She means 'cosy little nook' of course – it's like the kind of joke the guy dressed as a clown always used to make at birthday parties when I was little, and all the toddlers would fall about as if it was the funniest thing they'd ever, ever heard. Mrs Parsing calls them 'spoonerisms, a delightful play on words'.

'Teamwork is a wonderful thing for getting super ideas for stories,' Mrs Parsing was saying. 'That's how they write *The Simpsons*, you know. And after English, we're all going to hear some very exciting news from Miss Delaware.'

Miss Delaware is the drama teacher. She talks as if every other word is in italics and wears pink mohair jumpers and lipstick to match – pink, not hairy lipstick, that is. She looks like a lobster in lycra leggings. I've never seen any of her shows, but people say they're not as unusual as her appearance.

Then Mrs Parsing paired us off. I knew she would put me with Viola, and I couldn't see a way out of it. We sat side by side in stony silence until I felt a gentle tug on my sleeve and she passed me a note. It just said: *What's up*?

'Nothing,' I hissed.

'Why are you avoiding me? Is it something I've done?' she whispered.

All right. If she wanted the truth, I'd give it to her. Furiously, I scrawled: *You never got in touch the whole of Christmas. You never even sent a card. You never answered my messages. And you've been round to my house about* TEN TIMES *and never asked me back to yours. So you are not my friend any more.*

I glanced at her as she read it and she looked mortified. Then I saw a tear trickle down her cheek.

She wrote back: *I am sorry. I can explain. See you in the loos. Please.* I didn't have the heart to say no.

In the toilets she told me a whole lot of stuff that changed everything.

She said she HAD sent me a Christmas card. Secretly, I cursed Candice. She gets masses of mail about her gallery, but she's very disorganised and loses a lot of it, and everybody else's as well. Viola's card is probably still in a pile on her desk.

'I told you in the card that I'd be in Scotland for the whole holidays because my gran was poorly,' Viola said.

She paused to stare at her shoes, which she always does when she isn't sure what to say next, before whispering, 'I know it's bad about not asking you home, but Mum doesn't like people coming to the house.' Another pause. 'It gives her migraines.'

I wasn't sure I believed the last bit, but Viola looked so distraught and I had been so miserable all day with no one to talk to that I was really glad to accept what she said.

Final period was drama with Miss Delaware. She bounced pinkly into the room.

'Thrilling news,' she trilled. 'Year Seven are all getting together to do a musical for the Easter Term show. And it'll be our VERY OWN musical, written by Mr Simpkins!'

There was a mixture of groans, jeers and giggles at this. Miss Delaware has been seen out at candlelit dinners with Mr Simpkins, the music teacher, who fancies himself as the next Andrew Lloyd Webber.

'What about *West Side Story*?' Tobylerone demanded. 'My dad's got a great knife I could use for the fights.'

'Did it last year,' Miss Delaware said. 'Your brother ended up in hospital, if you remember.'

'*Bugsy Malone*!' somebody shouted.

'Babyish,' said Miss Delaware.

'*Oliver*!' said somebody else.

'Everybody else is doing it,' said Miss Delaware.

'The working title of this extravaganza is *Pirates and Aliens* although of course we will come up with something more dramatic soon,' Miss Delaware carried on.

'*Piraliens*,' said Eric Cubicle, who's very good at Scrabble.

'But that's rude, Miss,' said Tobylerone.

'What do you mean, Toby?'

'Well, calling people aliens. Just because they come from other countries, doesn't mean . . .'

Miss Delaware went as pink as her jumper.

'Toby. I THINK you know that we are talking about aliens from outer space. And pirates, of course, from, er, here.'

'Will we have a space rocket?' asked Nigel the geek.

'And a pirate ship? With rigging?' asked Malik.

'Does everyone have to sing? Because not everyone can,' said Sandra, who fancies herself as the next Charlotte Church.

'Too many questions,' said Miss Delaware, looking thrilled with the attention. 'But I can assure you this *wonderful* show will be a work of art soon, children, greater than all of us and deserving of a bigger stage. What a *shame* we have to squeeze such an epic into our little school hall.'

Well, Falmer North's hall is not that little, but it is horrible and flakey and is lit by a few forty-watt bulbs and has no proper stage because there is never enough money for art, as my adored mother Candice keeps on reminding me when she drones on about how lovely it would be if I could go to a posh school that understood real art like Shakespeare and Mozart instead of rappers and clowns playing musical saws. She has some funny ideas. I have never seen a clown playing a musical saw, not even at Falmer North.

Anyway, rehearsals for this great event, 'a swashbuckling tale of pirates on the seven seas and aliens from outer space', will begin next week.

'I suppose Johnny Depp has made pirates all the rage, but it sounds a bit childish,' I grumbled to Viola on the way home. 'It is so typical of grown-ups to think we would like to do pirates and aliens. And why does she say 'outer space'? Space is just space, isn't it?'

'You're very grumpy, I thought you liked adventure and romance.'

'I wish we were doing West Side Story,' I said.

'But the boys get all the good parts in that,' she said.

'What? What about Maria? And Anita? And best of all, Anybodys?'

'Who?'

And I realised she had never seen West Side Story, so I asked her home to see our old video. She wanted to be Maria. But of course I wanted to be Anybodys, the tomboy, who longs to be in the Jets.

Viola went home looking happier than I'd ever seen her, humming 'I Feel Pretty'.

It is so great being friends with her again.

After she'd left I phoned Callum to tell him we were friends again.

'Great. So has she asked you back to hers?'

'No. She says her mum gets migraines.'

'And you believe that?'

'Why not? People do get migraines. My mum always expects to if anything goes wrong, though they never quite turn up.'

Callum snorted. 'But it's just an excuse isn't it? She's got something to hide, so she makes sure nobody can get into the house.'

'Mmm. Maybe.'

'Look, I've got a half day for Founders' Day tomorrow. I

could hang about your school and trail you back to yours and then we could both stalk Viola.'

'We can't stalk my best mate! It doesn't feel right.'

'It's not exactly stalking, it's following. I'm interested in where Viola lives, too.'

I could almost hear Callum wishing he hadn't said that. Quickly he added, 'It'll be good for your story. And you're trying to help Viola, remember?'

I thought for a moment.

'You are a fawney-dropping flammy dollymop. But yes, let's go for it.'

As I put down the phone I realised I'd just called Callum something indescribably rude. I'd better watch out with this Victorian insult caper. I also felt a lurch of disloyalty towards Viola, as though I were betraying her somehow by spying on her.

Aunt Laura's words echoed in my head: *Remember, this isn't one of your stories, it's real life. If your friend wants to keep something private, it's her choice.*

But I told myself it was for Viola's own good. If her dad is in prison, she needs support and guidance. And anyway, it'll be fun to be detectives with Callum. Even if he is at an annoyingly posh school with things like Founders' Days, at least he hasn't changed towards me and still wants to have old-fashioned fun.

Next day, I got cold feet at going-home time in case Viola spotted Callum outside the school. She has met him once when we all went to the circus. But it was raining so hard you could hardly see anything anyway, and Callum was lurking outside the school gates disguised in his dad's old raincoat and shielding his face with an enormous bumbershoot. He looked a bit sinister hanging around like that.

But I could see he'd spotted us, so I scuttled off as quickly as possible, dragging Viola behind me with Callum loping along about twenty paces after us and stopping to do his shoelaces whenever we slowed down, just like a detective in a film. Viola slowed down quite a lot, as she is one of those people who does one thing at a time. She can't really walk and talk at once. I think it's because she's so intense. So whenever she wanted to say something, she paused in order to get the words out. We were getting stupidly wet as a result and I hurried her on. She stopped expectantly outside my house but I cruelly explained that my aunt was coming to tea and I couldn't ask her in.

She exploded with excitement. 'Your Aunt Laura? Oh, please, let me come in just for one second, just to glimpse her. PLEASE.'

Whoops.

'No, not that aunt. My other one. She's old and deaf and smells of cabbage,' I lied, frantically.

Viola looked hurt just the same but I stood my ground and she sloped off looking like a drowned mouse. I dashed inside to borrow one of Howard's big coats and, well-disguised and sheltered under Callum's massive bumbershoot, we stealthily followed our prey. It was a slow business.

'Bloody hell. She stops and starts a lot, doesn't she?' hissed Callum.

And it's true. Viola went even more slowly now she was not with me. She paused to look at things like leaves. I found myself thinking maybe she didn't want to go home, and it made me sad.

Finally we saw her turn off the main street. It was just as I suspected – she was heading for the roughest, mankiest estate in town. Local busybodies are always campaigning to shut down the Duchess Estate. It's a mean, cramped bunch of flats linked by filthy dark walkways and smelly tunnels where you expect to find muggers in every dank stairwell. One of my friends at primary school used to live here, and when Candice picked me up once from a Halloween party she made me promise never to set foot there again. All the flats and alleyways are named after lords and kings and earls, which makes it seem worse.

'It's going to be hard to follow her if she takes the lift,' mumbled Callum, hanging back. The same thought had occurred to me, so I was relieved when she started search-ing for her keys near a ground-floor flat. Viola looked round nervously as she made to open the door and Callum and I ducked down behind a burned-out wreck of a car. The Duchess is where all the joyriders dump their vehicles, according to Candice. Then came a big surprise. Just as Viola had opened the door, a tiny figure rocketed out and jumped on her.

'Vi, Vi!' it squeaked. 'I'm making a poo cake!'

Viola dropped her school bag and laughed. She gave the loony infant a hug and carried it inside.

'I didn't know she had a sister. Or is it a brother?' I said to Callum.

'The plot thickens,' he said.

We decided not to barge in right then. I needed to think of a good excuse to go round. But I felt better knowing where she lived. And worse, too, in a way. I really hope I am not a snob like Candice, but if I had to live on the Duchess, I think I would be a whole lot shyer and more nervous than Viola.

'I think she's kept quiet about where she lives, and maybe stuff about her dad too, because she wants to be someone else at school, you know – someone who can Be Something,' I said to Callum as we headed home.

'Why shouldn't she be someone and live on the Duchess?' he asked. 'Most great people had tough beginnings.'

The next day, I borrowed Viola's hairbrush at break and 'forgot' to give it back.

This was daft, since my hair is short spikes and doesn't see a hairbrush from one week to the next, but I needed something to borrow that she wouldn't miss too much, so I could have an excuse for 'dropping in'.

At about five p.m. I went round. I was dead nervous of leaving it any later as it was already dark and I didn't fancy walking round the Duchess too late. Very weedy, I thought to myself, since Viola has to live there all the time.

The minute Viola opened the door, I knew I shouldn't have come. She looked clammy with shock.

'Er, hi,' she said, after what seemed like hours. She'd only opened the door about five centimetres, and I couldn't see much of her except her little unhappy-vole face.

I stood there, waving her hairbrush stupidly. 'You . . . er . . . left this at school,' I stammered.

Viola looked at it as if it were some strange bristly creature she'd never seen before.

I wanted to give it to her and run away as far as I could, but the insane child Callum and I had glimpsed the previous day zoomed through the gap like electric toothpaste and clamped itself round my knees.

'Come in, come in, we're having tea with the Queen,' it squeaked.

Viola changed from white to scarlet. She stuttered something about her mum having a funny turn.

'No, it's OK, I can't stop, really,' I said. But Loony Tunes was hauling me in by my bag strap.

'Queen's tea! You must come!' it bellowed.

'Well, just for a minute,' I said, dreading what I was going to see.

I thought it would be like a telly documentary, with rats nibbling on unwashed plates, a drunken mum smoking and eating the cat's food, bottles and old fast-food wrappings everywhere. But the place was spotless. It was a tiny flat. I thought my bedroom was small, but you could have fitted most of Viola's flat into it. The whole place sparkled like it had been polished just that minute by the house-work fairy.

'Oh, what a lovely flat,' I shouted. But it had the right effect on Viola, who actually smiled.

The Queen's tea was laid out on a tiny table in front of the telly. It was a doll's tea set and a plate of biscuits with an assortment of toys sitting round. They were a hippo, a cushion with a face painted on it, a giraffe and a tractor.

'Good evening, Your Majesty,' I said, bowing to the giraffe, who looked the most regal.

'Snot the Queen, stupid. It's a giraffe,' said Loony Tunes in a very imperious voice. 'The Queen is coming at six-thirty so you'd better wash your face and brush your hair.'

'Don't be rude, Bugsy,' said Viola, relaxing. 'This is my best friend from school, Cordelia. And this is my little sister, Bugsy.'

I felt a warm glow as she said 'best friend' and wanted to hug her. I was also relieved to find out Bugsy was a sister. I'd have hated to make a mistake.

'And this is my mum. Mum – Cordelia.'

Viola's tiny, shy mum, who I had seen briefly at the circus, was peering anxiously in the doorway, wringing her hands.

I've only ever read about people doing this, and as A Famous Writer To Be, I'm glad to have seen it in real life. It looked like somebody trying to squeeze water out of some invisible washing. But then Viola's mum gave me the sweet-est smile.

'Viola's told me a lot about you. I'm so sorry you haven't been able to come round before when you've had her round so often,' she said. Viola was blushing furiously and staring at her shoes. 'Would you like a cup of tea? Or some lemonade? And a biscuit?'

She gestured to the sofa and I sat down carefully next to the tractor. Bugsy, who should obviously be the next head of the United Nations, went on breaking the ice brilliantly by introducing me to all the toys, so I had to shake their hooves, paws and wheels, which all took quite a long time, while Viola stared at her shoes and her mum whistled about in the kitchen and returned with a tray of biscuits and a jug of lemonade.

'I'm afraid we're a bit cramped here,' she said. 'I'd love Viola to have her own room, but she shares the sofa bed in here with Bugsy at the moment. It's much smaller than where we were before and we've put our names down for a bigger flat, but you know how it is.'

'Oh yes,' I lied, thinking of our own rambling house where Howard and Candice have a study each and we've got a big through-room and a separate kitchen and two bathrooms. I thought of Candice moaning about not having enough money and thought I was going to blush as hard as Viola. 'But it's a lovely flat, so pretty and cosy,' I said. Which was true. 'And I'm so sorry I couldn't come before. I've been meaning to, of course.'

Viola threw me a grateful smile. I realised that the reason I'd never been there was nothing to do with her mum's migraines, if she ever had any. Viola just hadn't wanted me to see where she lived. It was really daft of her of course, but I understood. I thought maybe I would feel just the same if I was her.

There was a wedding photo on the mantlepiece, showing Viola's mum arm in arm with a smiling young man.

'Is this your dad?' I asked Viola, before I could stop myself.

'That's right – wasn't he handsome?' said Viola's mum, quickly. 'He's away on business just now.'

There was a short silence. Viola was looking at her shoes again.

Then her mum said, 'I'll leave you two to chat now. Come and help me in the kitchen, Bugsy,' dragging the squawking Bugsy in her wake.

'But the Queen!' she yelled.

'Her Majesty is not due for another twenty minutes. Come and help peel the spuds.' She shut the door firmly behind her.

I turned to Viola. 'Your mum's lovely. She doesn't look like she has migraines. And why didn't you tell me about Bugsy? She's sooo sweet,' I said.

'She can be a complete pain,' said Viola. 'Sharing a room with a four-year-old means you don't sleep much, you can't watch TV after nine, and you usually wake up with a furry tractor on your head.' But she was laughing. 'I know I've been an idiot. I think I wanted to be mysterious. I wanted to be more like you. I thought, because you've got a big house and your parents are all artistic and you've got a famous writer for an aunt, that you wouldn't want to be my friend if you saw my place. I thought you'd go off me and your mum wouldn't want you coming here.'

She didn't know how right she was about the last bit, and I certainly wasn't going to tell her.

'You are a one hundred per cent idiot,' I said. 'Our house is a complete tip. At least you can't lose your homework here.'

'Because there's nowhere to lose it. But that means I don't have an excuse. Oh, it's so great you're here. It's really been bothering me, having to pretend.' Viola stretched out like a cat on the floor. Then suddenly she sat up, as if she had seen a ghost.

'Wait a minute. How did you know where I lived? You followed me, didn't you?'

'No!' I said, but I could feel myself reddening. 'I . . . er, asked Tobylerone.'

'Oh, yeah. I made him promise not to tell you.'

'But, you know, I needed to give you the hairbrush . . .'

To my relief, Viola decided to let it go.

'Now to the really important question. How's the writing going? What's your new story about?'

We chatted happily for a while and then a horrendous battering on the door made us realise it was time for the Queen's tea party. Viola jumped up giggling and opened the door, bowing low.

'She's not here yet, silly,' said Bugsy.

'Oh yes she is, she's behind you,' said Viola, just like in

a panto. 'Hurry up and get ready.'

Bugsy scuttled to the sofa and sat down next to the giraffe.

Viola's mum came back in ceremoniously carrying a teapot with a picture of the Queen on it. It looked ancient, like things my granny has from the Coronation. Not at all the kind of thing Candice would own, I thought. Or sell in her gallery, either.

I was about to say what a perfect teapot for the Queen's tea when I realised that it *was* the Queen, at least for the purposes of Bugsy's tea party.

We all got up and bowed.

'Would you like some tea, Your Maj?' asked Bugsy conversationally, curtseying to the teapot, and I had to hug Princess Cushion very hard to avoid spifflicating with giggles. Looking back on it, that little Queen's tea party was one of the nicest, friendliest teas I have ever had.

In fact, I'd entirely forgotten why I'd gone there in the first place, until something strange happened.

Viola had gone out to the kitchen to help her mum with the washing up, and when she was gone, Bugsy scrambled over to the sofa bed, opened a drawer underneath it, and pulled out a cardboard box. There were holes cut in it for windows. They had matchsticks glued across them, like bars. A little plastic figure sat inside. He was wearing overalls – he might have been a dustman or a builder from a toddler's playset. Bugsy rummaged under her bed and pulled out a model Superman.

'Is it a bird? Is it a plane?' Bugsy muttered to herself. 'Eeeeeaaayoowwww,' she went, swooping Superman over the box, picking up the figure inside, and carrying him off. She kept her arm stretched above her head, holding the two models, while she searched for something else.

'What are you looking for, Bugsy?' I said, giggling.

'Me, me,' said Bugsy, impatiently.

I tickled her under her outstretched arm. She wriggled away, but didn't laugh.

'But you're here,' I said to her. She shook her head and just jabbed her finger under the bed, and when I finally brought out a little plastic girl with yellow hair, she nodded furiously. I sat the little girl on the carpet, and Bugsy swooped Superman down in front of her. Then she moved the arms on the girl and the little man so they clung on to each other.

I began to understand what Bugsy meant.

'The little girl is you?' I asked. Bugsy nodded. 'And is the man your daddy?' She nodded again.

'In pwison. Superman will come and rescue him.' She paused, and scrutinised the caped figure. 'Or Batman. I don't mind.'

I suddenly realised that Viola and her mum were standing in the doorway, staring at us. I would like to have fallen into a very deep hole just then but there were no very deep holes in sight.

'Ha, ha, ha,' went Viola's mum.

'Ha, ha, ha,' went Viola.

'Ha, ha, ha,' went I.

Then I thanked them for the best tea of my life about a million times and escaped.

As I rushed away from Lord Stanley Court into Coronation Road I heard Viola shouting, 'Wait!' – she was running after me. I hurried on, pretending not to hear. I wanted everything to be as it was between us. I hated the thought that I'd embarrassed her.

'You've still got my hairbrush,' she shouted.

I stopped.

She caught up and looked at me seriously. 'It's true about my dad. You knew, didn't you?'

I nodded.

'Tobylerone told me, but he promised he'd never mention it to anyone else and I really don't think he will.'

'I know he won't,' said Viola. 'His dad's been inside too, so he knows how it is.'

She opened the locket that she always wears round her neck and revealed a really sweet picture of her dad, smiling. 'He's innocent,' she said.

'Of course he is,' I told her.

We're going to prove it. And we won't need Superman either.

When I got home there was an email from Callum. It was a whole lot of stuff about overcrowded prisons and the injustice of the system and horrible statistics about there being more prisoners in the UK than there had ever been before.

And there are a lot of mums in prison as well as dads. Some of them for really small things. And some are single parents! What's the point of that?

This is typical of Callum. When he wants to find out about something he is like a little terrier, burrowing away. He has a really weird obsession with statistics, or maybe it's not that weird, just a thing with boys. Even so, I'm grateful to him – I must tell Viola all this. I am determined to transform into Shirley, I mean Charlotte, Holmes myself and save the Larpent family from their doom on the Duchess Estate.

But meanwhile, here's Chapter Two of my fantastic soon-to-be-best-selling feminist detective melodrama. Maybe I'll change her name to Cordelia Holmes in the final version. Shame about Shirley.

> **Laura Hunt's Top Tips for Budding Writers:**
> Write as if you're telling a secret to a best friend.
>
> *That's easy, I do that in my diary. Goody – getting somewhere at last.*

The Bat of the D'Urbervilles (ctd)

'You may have read of the recent sad end of my uncle, Sir Roland D'Urberville,' Sir Horatio continued.

'I did observe some such account,' Charlotte Holmes said. 'He was found dead from a stroke, and the pulchritudinous pile of the D'Urbervilles now passes on to the next generation.'

'What the papers did not relate,' Sir Horatio said in a woebegone whisper, 'was that the stroke struck him on the stroke of midnight. Does that not strike you as strange?'

'Not at all,' Charlotte Holmes shot back sharply. 'Midnight is just a time like any other.'

'And it is not usual, is it, to find one's relative has a stake driven through his heart?'

'A little unusual, I will permit,' said Holmes, leaning forward just a bit. 'But I am sure there is some perfectly reasonable explanation.'

'Very well then,' whispered Sir Horatio yet more wanly, 'there is more.'

'Get on with it then, man,' snapped Dr Callum Watson, the man of action. 'We are busy, heroic types with not a minute to lose, and please speak up, your flimsy futile voice is fading fast.'

'The accounts also chose not to relate something much more spookily sinister,' said Sir Horatio, a bit louder. 'The servants at D'Urberville Hall have been terrified by the appearances of a giant bat, its claws dripping fire, its wings beating louder than the whirling blades of a helicopter. Sir Horatio faltered in his story before revealing that, beside the body of his uncle were two prints. 'They were like nothing I have ever seen on heaven or in Earth . . . great claws as of some gigantic bird of prey . . . only bigger, by far, than the biggest eagle.'

'Good God,' cried Watson, his simple face alight with alarm.

'Continue,' said Holmes, her bright eyes a shade brighter.

'For generations my family has been plagued by the curse of the giant bat of the D'Urbervilles. Each time a family member dies. Of course, I rejected these absurd stories as fantasy, BUT, I think I must tell you Holmes, that the first Earl of D'Urberville died in the most horrific circumstances – circumstances that would lead one to believe in the . . . dare I say it . . . supernatural.'

Holmes glanced at Watson, whose fine, thinning hair was standing on end. 'Poor Dr Watson,' she thought affectionately. 'He is prone to superstition, like so many men. I must protect him from these fears.'

But as Horatio D'Urberville continued, even Holmes herself felt the stirrings of deep profound unease.

Here was a dreadful tale indeed, the like of which even I, fearless Girl Writer Cordelia Arbuthnott, hesitate to set before my devoted readers for fear of driving them wailing into their mums' and dads' bedrooms in the small hours, seeking succour, security, snacks, sweeties, snuggles, soft toys, and everything else beginning with 's', no wait a minute, perhaps not everything . . .

Laura Hunt's Top Tips for Budding Writers:
Well-rounded characters will write your
story for you if you know them well enough
before you begin writing.

*What does 'well-rounded' actually mean? Not fat, obviously.
Does it mean you have to know what they like for breakfast?
I think maybe it does. OK. Charlotte Holmes would like
smoked salmon and lightly scrambled egg with a shot of
vodka. Dr Callum Watson would be a sausage-and-bacon
man. With tea you can stand your spoon in. Now I'm too
hungry to write another word.*

Chapter Three

Laura Hunt's Top Tips for Budding Writers:
Try to make use of all five senses when you're writing. How do things look, smell, taste, feel, sound?

Have tried hard, but can only think of sizzling sound, smell and taste of sausages, scrambled egg with beans and hot choccy with whipped cream. Also, how hot choccy looks in one of Candice's mugs shaped like a pair of shorts. Also, how it feels sliding down my throat. Perhaps I am too superficial, after all, to sit in the famed halls of writing . . .

Dear Aunt Laura,
Do you ever get the thing when you really want to get on with writing your story but you can't concentrate because of other things that are happening in your life?

Also, which can be even more difficult, do you have tips for when your friend is talking to you and you don't listen to them properly because you are busy imagining stories?

Do you have any tips on how to concentrate on the story

you're writing and forget everything else? And on how to
concentrate on real life and science lessons when you're really
thinking about your story?

What I need is three little bottles of potion: one for
concentrating on my story and actually getting down to
writing it; one for concentrating on lessons and boring stuff;
and one for concentrating on listening to incredibly
important real-life things.

Also, do the Three Bees ever say really embarrassing
things just when you don't want them to?
Love,
Cordelia

Don't know why I wrote this, but it made me feel better.
Probably won't send it.

I couldn't wait for school next day so I could tell Viola all
the prison stuff Callum had sent me.

But when I did, Viola was upset that I had told Callum
about her dad. I spent a while persuading her that it was
because he was my only other best friend apart from her,
and I was worried about her and didn't know who else to talk
to, and that I knew he wouldn't tell a soul. She did get interested in some of the things Callum had found out.

'You see?' I said to Viola, as we walked around the playground arm in arm. 'It's not just your dad. There are loads
and loads of mums and dads in prison. Some of them
have done something awful and have to be there. But
some of them have done something stupid just the once,

or maybe done nothing at all. Like your dad.'

'It's OK,' she said, after a bit. 'It's a relief to talk, really. Like having a horrible toothache and finally going to the dentist. I can't talk to Mum about it any more. She hasn't even taken me and Bugsy to see Dad recently. I think she's given up on him.'

'Why? If he's innocent?'

Viola looked at her shoes. Her fair hair fell like a curtain in front of her face.

'How does your hair do that when you don't want to say anything?' I asked. 'Mine's like hedgehog spikes, and when it's more than five centimetres long it's like a mushroom. But I can't be bothered with all that styling and pratting about in front of mirrors, can you?'

I drifted off for a few minutes thinking about hair and imagining that Viola was Rapunzel and Callum was climbing up her hair to rescue her from the tower. I didn't like the idea of Callum rescuing Viola very much and I snapped myself out of my daydream and realised Viola had been talking.

'Sorry, can you repeat that? It was a bit complicated.'

She sighed. She is used to me drifting off. She does it herself. I think all great writers do.

'I was trying to tell you what happened,' said Viola.

'Sorry,' I said.

'They called my dad Fizzy Oakes, right?'

I couldn't help giggling.

'That's a daft name,' I said.

'Thanks. The Fizzy part is because he was always laughing and joking,' (Viola gave a little sniff at this point, and I gave her arm an extra squeeze) 'and the Oakes is because he's so strong. He was sent to prison for a robbery he didn't do.'

'You can appeal or something, can't you?' I asked her. 'They have to do the case all over again.'

'I kept trying to persuade Mum to fight for that,' Viola said gloomily. 'But her heart wasn't in it. I don't think she believes he's innocent. And now she wants a divorce.'

Oh, poor Viola.

'I'm sure the truth would come out if we could only track down the real criminal,' she said. 'Dad says if he were free, he is sure he could find him.'

'Well then, let's spring him from jail!' I said, feeling the light of high adventure leaping in my soul. 'Come round to mine tomorrow and I'll get Callum round too. He's brilliant at hatching plots. There must be some way we can do it, like in all those escape movies.'

'I don't think I've ever seen an escape movie,' said Viola, 'and you've never been inside a prison. No offence, but it's not like the cartoons, you know. You can't just smuggle a file in inside a cake, so he can saw through the bars.'

'I know that, but either we do nothing and life goes on as it is, and your dad stays in jail, and your mum gets divorced, or we can do something. It's worth it, even if we end up in jail ourselves. And anyway we're too young for prison, so we can get away with anything.'

'You obviously haven't been inside a Young Offenders' Institution either,' said Viola darkly.

'Why, do you know someone who has?'

'No! I just read about them,' she snapped, reddening.

'Erm, isn't there any way we could free him? There must be a way.'

'He is allowed out once a week to attend classes, on account of good behaviour . . .'

'Well, that's a start.'

We had been so involved in our chat that we were a quarter of an hour late for the big casting session for the musical. We dashed into the gym to find Miss Delaware standing by a vast pile of what looked like several hundred giant, lime-green squid.

Tobylerone was lurching about doing his best croaky-voiced Jack Sparrow impression from *Pirates of the Caribbean*, because he'd just been made pirate chief.

To our horror, we found that all the pirate parts had been cast already and that the lime-green squid were the alien-from-outer-space costumes.

'She got them on eBay,' said Jolene.

'They must have paid her to take them away,' sniggered Zandra.

'We've got to wear them,' wailed Jolene. 'Ohmigod, it's so uncool.'

'I'm not wearing that,' I said.

'I will inform Mrs Warren of your lateness, girls, but you

still have time to audition for the part of the maiden who gets tied to the mast by the pirates and rescued by the aliens,' said Miss Delaware.

'It's got to be Viola,' said Tobylerone. 'She looks exactly right.'

Everyone turned to look at the blushing Viola, who squeaked that she couldn't possibly, but we all realised that with her huge eyes and long fair hair and constant expression of terror, she'd be just perfect.

'Good idea, Toby,' said Miss Delaware. 'It's all right, Viola, you don't have to do anything but sob a bit and then swoon into the alien chief's tentacles.'

Eric Cubicle, who looks like an alien anyway, had been cast as the alien chief. He waved his arms about and went 'woooo, wooooo' to Viola, to establish his identity. Viola's giggles broke out at that – it was really nice to see her amused for a change.

'Yes, Eric,' sighed Miss Delaware, 'but I think the alien chief represents a super-intelligent race, he's not a special effect from Dr Who.'

'Hang on a minute, don't I get to change sides and rescue her?' asked Tobylerone.

'Well, yes, at the very end, of course, the pirate chief has a change of heart and rescues you back from the aliens,' said Miss Delaware. 'But you still don't have to speak. You just smile happily as the pirates sing the finale.'

'I suppose it's better than wearing a tentacle suit,' Viola said, stifling her giggles.

This left me as an alien as far as I could see, and I didn't like it.

'Miss Delaware, no offence, but isn't it incredibly sexist to let the boys be pirates in nice waistcoats and hooks and peg legs while we have to wear these stupid, I mean, strange, suits? There were plenty of women pirates,' I added wildly.

'There were a couple of famous women pirates, Cordelia, that is true, and if you had been here on time, you might well have been one of them. Important as you are, you must realise that there are one hundred and fifty students in Year Seven and each of them has a part to play! I have given thirty pirate roles to boys and thirty to girls. Apart from our wonderful backstage boys and girls and our fabulous scene painters, the rest of you must be aliens.'

'Oh,' I said, deflated.

'But cheer up, the devil has the best tunes and I think the aliens have the best songs. Although *all* the songs are wonderful, of course,' she added, glancing at Mr Simpkins who was sitting patiently at the piano. 'Now, on with the motley!'

Everyone looked blank. Miss Delaware sighed.

'It's what they said in Shakespeare's time. It means putting on your costume, getting into your part.'

I made a mental note of this. It could come in handy when I write a novel about swashbuckling heroes and noble deeds set in whatever century Shakespeare hung out in.

'I know it's a bit early to get into costume but it will give us a *feel* for the show,' trilled Miss Delaware as, groaning and protesting, everybody went off to the changing rooms to get into the naff costumes, and came back, still moaning, in ones and twos. Eric Cubicle had his alien-chief costume on backwards – all the tentacles trailed along behind him, so everybody else kept standing on them while he tried to work out why he wasn't getting anywhere. For a very brainy person, he seems to have a lot of blank space in his head. Tobylerone looked great, I had to admit, with his eye-patch and wooden leg – even though his real leg was sticking out pretty obviously behind him with a trainer on the end, and the parrot sewn on his shoulder was hanging upside down on what remained of the thread.

When everyone had finally showed up, Miss Delaware gave us all the first act, and Mr Simpkins started introducing the opening song. Nobody knew how it went, and the school piano is very out of tune, so some people sang it to their favourite pop song, some people to their ring tones, some people just shouted. Miss Delaware went pale, but Mr Simpkins smiled happily and pounded on.

Viola then had to sing to herself while pretending to do her washing in an imaginary stream, and then scream loudly when captured by the pirates led by Tobylerone.

'Ow!' said Viola, as the pirates tied her to the wall bars, which were supposed to represent a ship's mast. 'I can't breathe.'

'Avast, my pretty,' Tobylerone hissed, 'you are our prisoner, so stop moaning, innit.'

Eric Cubicle leaped forward heroically at this point, but

somebody had tied a tentacle to the vaulting horse, and he fell flat on his face.

'Mmmmph,' said Eric, or something of that sort.

'Not yet, Eric,' said Miss Delaware. 'You don't come on until the second act.'

It all went from bad to worse from there. The pirates with wooden legs kept complaining of cramp and kept having to be massaged, everyone kept treading on each other's tentacles even when they didn't mean to, so people started tying them up round their waists like the sleeves of jumpers, mobile phones went off, some people started playing baseball with a wooden leg, and eventually a despairing Miss Delaware gave up and told us to come back tomorrow. She had to shout at Mr Simpkins, still smiling happily, to stop him playing the piano.

'It was important to get a feel of the costumes at an early stage, but we will rehearse in tracksuits and trainers from now on, to get you into your parts,' were her final despondent words as we trooped out.

'I've never seen anything so ridiculous in my life,' I said to Viola on the way home.

'Yeah, I'm glad I don't have to dress up as a squid,' she laughed.

'I've texted Callum to devise a plan about freeing your dad. He's brilliant at plans. Look what he texted back,' I said. And showed her:

No Prob, C U in tree tomorrow. 6.00.

All Viola said was, 'TREE?'

Of course, I wanted to help Viola more than anything. But I had a nagging doubt. People always believe their own dad is innocent, don't they? Now I had her dad's nickname – not Dizzy Stokes, as I'd thought, but Fizzy Oaks – I reckoned I should try that out on the internet.

That evening, feeling really nervous, I typed 'Fizzy Oaks' into Google Advanced Search. Looking back at that moment, I knew I didn't want to find out anything bad about Viola's dad, I really wanted to believe he was innocent. So it was a huge relief to me when nothing came up. Not even a trial report.

I phoned Callum to tell him about the nickname.

'Well, that's not going to work, is it?' he said. 'It'll only be other criminals who know his nickname, won't it?'

'Yes, but when we tried Larpent nothing came up either . . .'

'Hmmm. A mystery. Which will be solved when we free him! See you tomorrow.'

I slept really badly. I knew I wanted to free Viola's dad, but I was scared we might be letting a dangerous criminal loose . . .

I didn't fill Viola in on the details of our tree. I wanted it to be a surprise. So at the appointed time, we showed up in Callum's garden, and Viola eagerly followed me up the ladder into the tree house. Callum hadn't arrived yet, of course.

'Cool,' said Viola. She tried to stroke Callum's cat Einstein, who had been sleeping on the pile of old coats, but he just

growled and meandered off grumpily. 'I wish I had somewhere like this. It's great to have somewhere private you can
just go and think. All the secret places where I live smell of
wee, or have a Rottweiler living in them, not a cat.'

'We're supposed to have grown out of tree houses, that's
what my mum says,' I told Viola.

'That's the trouble with grown-ups,' she said. 'They forget
how to have any fun.'

Callum finally arrived. His plan went like this: once we
found the place where Viola's dad was going to be taken for
his course we would wait there for the prison van to arrive.
Then we would stage a diversion.

'Er, what kind of diversion?' I asked.

'I haven't worked it out completely yet. But something
like this. The only thing we'll need will be a lot of fake blood
and a knife. We wait until the prison van draws up outside
the Adult Learning Institute, and then, just as they unload
the prisoners, you'll rollerblade straight into them screaming blue murder. You have to say something like, "Help! He's
going to kill me!" Then I rush up and stab you, which bursts
the fake blood bags that you'll be wearing under your sweat-
shirt. There will be loads of blood so it will look very
realistic. You fall over dead. Viola runs up screaming, "He's
murdered her! My best friend! Catch him!" Then most of the
guards run after me and in the confusion Viola grabs her
dad. We maybe need Tobylerone's big brother to be there
too, because he can drive. We do need a getaway car . . .'

Callum ground to a halt.

Viola and I stared at him.

There was a long silence.

'What's wrong?' asked Callum.

'All of it,' I said. 'None of it could possibly work. These are real prison guards in charge of real prisoners, they're not going to be fooled by three eleven-year-olds on rollerblades and a bucket of fake blood. And why would Tobylerone's brother want to get himself killed in a police chase for our sake?'

Viola's hair had fallen like a curtain. 'Never mind, she said. It was sweet of you to try,' and she gave Callum one of her sunshine-bursting-through-clouds smiles.

I blamed myself. I had honestly thought Callum would have some fantastic idea. I always think real life is going to be like a book, or a film. And it never is.

I wrote a lot that night, so here it is:

The Bat of the D'Urbervilles (ctd)

Horatio continued, his voice all atremble, as he unrolled an old murky, mildewed manuscript that had been secreted by his ancient ancestors in the wine cellars of D'Urberville Hall.

'Vladimir, the first Earl of D'Urberville, was crazed with passion for a young serving girl. One day, drunk, he kidnapped her and took her home. Locking her in the attic, he drunkenly dallied and danced with his friends, boasting of his success in capturing the maid. They did not believe him and so he bade them come and look. On hearing the drunken, oafish shouts of many men upon the stairs, the poor girl, nearly dead of fright, made fast the door with a great bolt. It took the feverish fellows many minutes to batter down the door and when they entered, the bird had flown. Naught but an open window showed she had been there, and the tiny attic room that had served as her prison was swathed in a dank, damp, drifting fog, which had drifted in through the window from whence she had leaped.

'"Alas! She will be dead!" cried the heart-broken but wicked Earl. However, there was no trace of the maid below, for she had swiftly climbed down the thick ivy that covered the walls of the ancient stately pile where the D'Urbervilles were to live for many generations, each of them cursed . . .

'The first Earl, wild with a frenzy of passion, mounted his coal-black steed and set off in hot pursuit after the innocent serving maid. His friends followed fast, on their more ordinary horses.

'They galloped across the impenetrable fog-bound misty moorland for many miles and then heard a sound that froze their very blood – a screeching, scary scream that penetrated the thick fog on the cold capacious moor. But that hair-raising, horrifying howl was as nothing compared to the sound that followed: a high-pitched squeal as of some ominous creature and the steady, fierce flapping of gigantic wings . . .'

Charlotte Holmes interrupted Sir Horatio's terrible, terrifying tale.

'This is all well and good if you like scary stories of

ghoulies and ghosties,' she enunciated eloquently. 'But the villains we valiantly vanquish are flesh and blood, and live in the same world as you and me. These are fairy stories for ignorant infants and superstitious sub-species.'

'Wait a moment, Charlotte Holmes,' said Sir Horatio, 'the story continues and you may find it has more in common with the sad end of my uncle, Sir Roland, than you think.'

Sir Horatio continued, 'Most of the Earl's comrades fled at the scary sounds, but two brave and loyal servants urged their terrified steeds forward. A sight met their eyes that can barely be described. The serving girl lay dead, her neck broken, like a broken-necked doll. Beside her, another body lay and, crouching over it, glowing with a green fire from hell, was a huge bat, at least eight foot long and with a wingspan of maybe twenty feet.

'The bat turned and stared at the men with its luminous red pulsating eyes and its cavernous jaws ringed with fangs of flame and then, very slowly, for it had done its work for the night, it rose into the air and drifted away, laughing a high-pitched cackle like the very devil himself. When the trembling servants approached the body of Vladimir D'Urberville (for it was he) they found it drained not only of life, but of all blood. He had become a lifeless thing, a transparent ghoul. The marks of the bat's fangs were deep in his neck. And a STAKE was driven through his heart.'

Phew. Have now scared myself with this. For once, I am glad to have Xerxes on my bed . . .

Laura Hunt's Top Tips for Budding Writers:
Stuck for a subject? Why not use an
exciting newspaper headline as a starting
point for your own original story?

NUDE VICAR CARTWHEELS DOWN HIGH STREET
will not go down well with Mrs Parsing.

Chapter Four

Laura Hunt's Top Tips for Budding Writers:
To make dialogue sound realistic, listen
to how your friends and family speak.

*If I used the language I heard in the loos at Falmer North
nobody would print this book.*

Miss Delaware's and Mr Simpkins's terrible musical is now called *Maiden at the Mast*.

The plot (I think) goes like this: Helpless Maiden (Viola) doing her washing by the stream gets captured by pirates and taken off to their island lair, where they spend all their time drinking rum, fighting, leering at Helpless Maiden and going 'Yo Ho Ho!'.

When they're not doing that, they're fighting the Indians – Native American ones, not Asian ones – who live on another part of the island. This bit has been shamelessly nicked from *Peter Pan*, but it all has to happen off-stage to a few random drumbeats, warbling sounds and more 'Yo Ho Hos', because we haven't got any American Indian costumes apart from the odd feather.

In the second act, strange coloured lights start appearing in the sky and weird noises are heard. This part is down to Mr Giggs, the IT teacher, who is apparently working out an amazing programme that could probably do the effects for *Lord of the Rings* let alone *Maiden at the Mast*. His computer keeps crashing at the moment, though, so we're having to imagine that part.

The pirates get very scared about the lights and noises, drink a lot more rum, and all fall asleep. The noise of a spacecraft landing (Mr Giggs says he's particularly proud of this one) is heard, and Eric Cubicle and his green aliens arrive. Viola, thinking things are going from bad to worse, starts to scream – but the alien chief freezes her to the spot with her mouth open. He then tells her he means no harm, and is going to set her free, and all the aliens squelch about doing a chorus as the climax of the first half.

Miss Delaware got rather cross when we all asked her why the alien speaks English, but Eric Cubicle is pretty hard to understand anyway, especially inside his alien suit, so what he says comes out something like, 'Urgle flarp tweedle gloop mneayh mneayh', and is therefore alien enough for anybody, I would have said, even if the audience won't have much idea what's happening.

It's pretty vague what happens after the interval, too. I don't think Miss Delaware and Mr Simpkins have quite worked it out. Maybe they get distracted by the stuff Tobylerone says they get up to in Mr Simpkins's car after school, and which I'm afraid I can't put in this family book.

There's supposed to be a big fight between the aliens and the pirates, with the invisible Indians joining in on the alien side, and then at the end everybody sings a song about how we're all the same really, whether we've got wooden legs, or tentacles or green skins, and the important thing is to forget our differences and Save the Planet. Eeeek.

We've been doing the stuff up to the aliens' arrival all week; I think they're stalling us while they try and write the last part. Why don't they ask me? I could have written a much better play than this pile of old poo, and there would-n't have been any green alien costumes to humiliate everybody either. But on our last rehearsal of the week, the play did get a lot more dramatic, though not because of any-thing Miss Delaware and Mr Simpkins had put in it.

Viola, the sweet, innocent girl tied to the mast of the pirate ship, was straining at her bonds and suddenly burst into violent floods of tears.

Miss Delaware shrieked with excitement and clapped her hands. 'Viola! *Wonderful*! What a *fabulous* performance! A star is born!'

Maybe all drama teachers are a bit over the top, but hon-estly the way Miss Delaware praises Viola is going to give her a bad name for favouritism. Also, I could see Viola wasn't acting. This was for real.

'That's marvellous dear, but that's enough now, we must leave room for Captain Crook to speak . . .'

Tobylerone, who insisted on wearing his peg leg through-out rehearsals to get into the part, was shifting embarrassedly from foot to peg and back, partly because he'd also realised Viola was *really* crying, and partly because he was trying to keep his wooden leg from falling off. Viola was now sobbing uncontrollably. I ran on stage towards her.

'Viola, what's wrong? Please tell me!' I said, trying to get her to look at me. But she wouldn't.

'Erm, I think Viola's thrown herself a little too much into the role. Let's all take a weeny break,' said Miss Delaware, finally seeing the light.

I shepherded Viola off into the loos.

She now had those horrible hiccups you get when you just can't stop crying. Several tissues later, she hiccupped herself to a standstill.

'It's all your fault,' she finally said, gulping.

'Why? What have I done?'

'Why did you raise my hopes about freeing my dad? With such a dumb idea? We were getting along OK until you put your big oar in.'

I could see she was getting really angry now. So was I.

'I was only trying to help, but if that's how you feel I'll leave you to it,' I said, and stomped out.

I was furious. I was so furious with Viola I never wanted to speak to her again. I didn't care if she was upset – I was upset too. After all I had done, why didn't she realise how much I cared?

But it turned out I didn't have to bother ignoring Viola the next week, because SHE ignored ME. Worse, she went and sat with the banshees and started giggling in lessons.

She even talked back to Mrs Parsing in English and said what was the point of writing stories when there were too many books in the world anyway and they were all for stuck up middle-class kids, and she looked pointedly at ME when she said it, and Jolene and Zandra sniggered.

So now I am alone again with my Art. I am trying to write my story but it is all dust and ashes. Why can't real life be more like stories and have happy endings? Why couldn't we have rescued the prisoner like Charlotte Holmes would?

Laura Hunt's Top Tips for Budding Writers:
You've sat and stared at a blank page for hours and you just can't get anything down. Why not try a completely different angle? How about a poem? It could be a long narrative poem, like 'The Ancient Mariner', or a little limerick, in the style of Edward Lear. Anything will help get you started!

Hmmm.
There was a young sleuth in a hat
Who was very intrigued by a bat.
There were flapping wings
And all sorts of things
That made her exclaim, 'Fancy that!'
Not sure this is my thing, really, but have hopes.

Dear Aunt Laura,

I hope you are well, and the Three Bees
and Joan and Joan. Well, as you know, I
never write unless I've got a problem,
so here goes. I have been trying and
trying to help my friend whose dad is in
jail, and she has told me to stop
shoving my big oar in. Now she hasn't
spoken to me for THREE DAYS. Don't you
think that's incredibly mean?

But worse, I think it has completely
changed her character. I think she has
decided to be cool and naughty and sit
with the bad kids and not do any work.
And maybe it's all MY FAULT. If only I
could prove her dad is innocent, then
maybe she would be my friend again and
not end up a drug addict from a broken
home.

Help!

xxC

Laura emailed me back within the hour.

Darling Cordy,

My sympathies, sweetheart. It's
miserable when your best friend turns
against you. I do see, reading between

the lines, that you ignored my earlier
advice not to be a nosey parker, but
I'm not surprised. I admire you for
trying to help, and to be honest, I
think I'd have done the same when I was
your age.

However, I think you are being a
teensy bit melodramatic!! Just because
Viola hasn't spoken to you for a couple
of days doesn't mean she has forgotten
you. Nor does it mean she is going to
end up living on the streets! She is
merely trying to spread her wings and
make some new friends and show she can
be a little more independent, which is a
good thing. Imagine how insecure this
whole business has made her - not to
mention her being very upset about her
father in the first place.

Try to understand how she feels and
give her a little space and I'm sure
she'll come back to you. Meanwhile, if
you really do want to pursue the
question of her father's innocence - and
I'm not sure I advise it - then why not
do a little sleuthing yourself? It will
be good for your detective story.
Research is just as important a skill

```
for the writer as knowing how to write
thrilling and inspiring words! And doing
some research will also stop you feeling
so sorry for yourself!!
    Absolutely oooodles of love and do
hope you'll come up and visit soon.
    Your adoring auntie xxxxxxxx xxxxxxxx
xxxxxxxxxxxxxxxxxxxxxxxxxxxxxxxxxxxxxxxxxx
xxxxxxxx(xxxx)
```

Sorry for myself? What a cheek! All right, I WILL be a sleuth.
I WILL uncover the secret of Viola's dad, and just now I don't
care if he's a mass murderer as long as I can find out the
TRUTH. In fact, I hope he is a mass murderer – it'll serve
Viola right.

But it was a bit hard to know where to start. Candice was
out that night at her book group (she says nobody reads the
book, they just gossip and talk about how clever or hopeless
their kids are) so I sat down to fish fingers with Howard.
That's his regular diet when Candice isn't around.

'You writing at the moment, Cord?' Howard asked me. He
does take an interest in my dreams of being an author. I
think he fancied being one himself once.

'Yes, Dad, I'm writing a kind of Sherlock Holmes detective
story, with violins and gas lamps and fog and villainous ras-
cals and stuff.'

'Sounds great,' Howard said. 'Sorry the fish fingers are a
bit black.'

'How did Sherlock Holmes know so much, Dad?' I asked, cutting off the black bits.

Howard chortled. 'Well, of course Holmes knew so much because he knew everything. And he also discarded anything he didn't think he needed to know. There's a marvellous passage in one of the books, I forget which, where Dr Watson tells Holmes about the earth going round the sun or something like that, which every five-year-old knows today, and Holmes just replies that he will try to forget that piece of useless information as soon as possible.'

He got up and rummaged around in the bookshelves.

'Here it is,' he said, and read:

'What the deuce is it to me?' he interrupted impatiently; 'you say that we go round the sun. If we went round the moon it would not make a pennyworth of difference to me or to my work.'

There was a whole lot more stuff about how the brain can only hold so much information, so you have to just keep what you need and throw out the useless bits, like clearing out an old attic.

After Howard had finished, I thought about this for a bit.

'I don't see why that's good. He might need to know about the sun someday. For timing, or shadows, or something.'

'Yes and of course it's very bad advice for anyone your age, because you have no idea what might come in useful,' Howard said, hastily. 'That's why you must concentrate very hard on what your teachers tell you even if it seems very

stupid. Obviously, Holmes just thought that too much information would clutter up his brain, which needed to be nice
and orderly, like a stationery cupboard where you know
exactly where everything is.'

'I wish my brain was like that,' I said.

'Hmmmm. And the house, too,' said Howard, sighing.

I looked around: the piles of books and newspapers and
teapots and vases and saucers and cups does seem to be
growing.

'Of course, your mum always says she's the only one in
the house who ever tidies up.' Howard sighed again.

'But not very often,' I said.

'Not very often is better than never. Now get on with your
homework.'

'Sherlock Holmes didn't have the internet, right?' I continued, pretending I hadn't heard the homework part.

'Of course he didn't, you noodle,' Howard said. 'They'd
hardly invented electricity when he was around, let alone
computers.'

'OK, so where would he have gone for information?'

'You ever heard of books?' Howard asked sarcastically,
pushing back his chair. 'Libraries? Newspapers?'

'Er, yes,' I said.

'Those were the things he built up his vast knowledge
from. He was highly educated in stuff relating to crime, and
he didn't seem to forget anything he needed to know. And
although he was a loner, he knew when to ask for help. I
think he reckoned the cops were mostly dumb, which was a

bit unfair, but he had a few useful contacts among the brighter ones.'

The police! How stupid of me!

'That's a good idea, Dad,' I said. 'I'll go and do my home-work now.'

'What's a good idea?' Howard called after me.

'The cops,' I said. 'I know just the person who can help with my story.'

The first person I could ask for help would be PC Budakli.

Next morning, he was on community-cop duty at school, as he usually is now. This is a new thing where the friendly bobby on the beat helps the kids to get to school safely and hopes to get to know the troublemakers by lurking around with a winning smile and an open, friendly manner, which is hard to do in a police uniform. Poor old cops: once kids get to secondary school they hate the police because the police are always nagging them and moving them on and assuming that any more than three kids walking along together is a gang. So PC Budakli looked like he'd won the lottery when I actually went up and talked to him.

Not expecting he'd know anything about it, I asked him if he'd ever heard the name Fizzy Oaks.

'Not a name you forget, is it?' PC Budakli said. 'My mate Alf, PC Butt that is – no laughing – was in the team that nicked him. It was quite big news at the time.'

I couldn't believe my luck.

'Why do you want to know, anyway?' PC Budakli smiled.

'Oh, we're doing a school project about crime and police work in the area,' I said quickly. 'I heard that name from somewhere, and it sounded exciting. Like somebody out of a story.'

'I'd be happy to talk to your class about police work,' PC Budakli said, looking pleased.

'Er, yes, that would be great,' I spluttered. 'But just for now, it's all down to what we can find out on our own.'

'Well, you can probably look it all up at the *Gazette* office,' the policeman said. 'It was in the autumn of 2004, as I remember – up in Stanford, where Alf and I used to be posted. 'Course, dear old Mrs Armitage was the key witness.'

'Mrs Armitage?'

'The original battling granny,' PC Budakli laughed. 'Old Fizzy could never have been identified from the CCTV – he had a stocking mask on. But Mrs Armitage was in the bank when it happened, tripped him up with her umbrella and pulled off his mask too. Amazing. She was the chief witness, and a bunch of England football fans who had just come out of the pub. They'd had a few beers, but they were pretty sure when it came to the identity parade, and Mrs Armitage clinched it.'

'Does she still live round there?' I asked, with my fingers crossed.

'Still runs a needlework shop in Stanford High Street,' PC Budakli said. 'Well, I'd better be getting on. Let me know if you want me to talk to your class. Any time.'

Of course, I got a lot of attention at break time after talking to PC Budakli. Everyone thought I'd been shoplifting. I didn't exactly deny it, as I wanted to seem interesting for once.

After school, I went to the office of the *Falmer Gazette*. The receptionist didn't look too pleased to be interrupted in a long phone conversation with somebody about the boring details of her wedding dress, but when I said I was doing a school project and wanted to see their back issues, she waved me in the direction of a bent old man who was sweeping up.

'Hello,' I said to him, 'I'm Cordelia, from Falmer North School. We're doing a local history project, and I'd like to see your back issues from summer 2004.'

'Know what you're looking for?' the old man asked.

'There was a bank robbery in Stanford then. An old lady helped catch the crook.'

He laughed a creaking-drawbridge laugh. 'Fizzy Oakes,' he said.

'You know about it?'

'Oh yeah – I remember everything. I'll show you the papers.'

We went downstairs into a big dusty cellar, where the back issues of the *Falmer Gazette* were bound into huge, leather-covered books. I looked around the shelves.

'Gosh,' I said to the old man. 'That one says 1867.' Howard was right. This was where I could get all the period detail for The Greatest Victorian Crime Novel Ever.

'Bit before my time, though you might not believe it,' he wheezed. 'Here's 2004. The robbery was around October, I think. 'Course, I could show you some other stuff much more interesting than that. There's the story I did when the last tram ran from Falmer West to Little Slaughter. Or the time Farmer Clackett's bull ran down the High Street and tried to get on a bus. Or when it turned out that Mr Thynne, the magistrate, had really been a woman all along . . . or . . .'

Fortunately, the receptionist was calling him back upstairs. He wheezed off, and I turned to October in the big leather book.

And there it was, October 16th, three years ago. Two days after the robbery. A huge photofit picture that looked exactly like Viola's dad (or at least, like the wedding photo I had seen). His name was not Larpent, of course, but Daniels. I guessed either Viola's mum was using her own family name so that the kids wouldn't be associated with a criminal dad, or maybe she had even changed her name. But it explained my failure with the internet. Maybe history teachers have a point when they tell you to go to real sources . . .

I looked at the next few editions of the *Gazette* and found another picture of Viola's dad being led away from the court by a policeman. And a sad little picture of Viola's mum, clutching baby Bugsy. LOCAL BOY MAKES BAD – FATHER OF TWO FIZZY OAKES UNDER ARREST.

Right. Fizzy O*akes*. Not Fizzy O*aks*, which is what I had typed into Google. Stupid of me, but I bet you'd have made the same mistake – after all, Viola had said he was called

'Fizzy' because he was funny and 'Oaks' because he was strong.

But worse was to come. When I read the trial report I felt very shaky. First, he'd had a gun! Thinking about it later, I realised that you probably need to have a gun to rob a bank, but it made me feel horrible, because Viola hadn't mentioned that bit. However, it got a lot worse after that. Reading on, I found this wasn't Viola's dad's first brush with the law, by any means. He'd been cautioned and done community service for loads of petty crimes, starting when he was at school! That's why the judge had given him fifteen years – because he was 'not of good character'.

It didn't seem very likely that Viola's dad was innocent of the bank robbery, after all. It seemed more likely that he'd done what criminals nearly always do: started small then moved on to bigger things.

I went back upstairs in despair. Viola was already not speaking to me. How would she take this piece of news? Or did she know it already?

The receptionist was still talking about her wedding dress on the phone. The old man winked. And then my eye fell on something utterly amazing. This week's edition of the *Falmer Gazette* was lying on a desk near the door. On its front page was a picture that almost made my eyes pop out of my head.

'Can I take this?' I squeaked to the old man. The receptionist kept on talking, but shook her head at me.

'Office copy,' said the old man. 'You'll have to get one at the newsagent.'

I shot out of the door, shouting 'Thanks!' to him as I ran.

I was out of there and into the shop in seconds, bursting with excitement. I bought the paper, and then I went straight round to Callum's.

'I think we need to be in the tree house. I've got something amazing to show you and I don't want anyone to see,' I said.

We clambered into the branches.

'Look!' I said, smoothing out the paper.

The front-page story was about Sir Alex King – a shipping millionaire who has just moved back to our town, where he had lived as a boy.

'What's so exciting about that?' asked Callum, grumpily.

'The photo! Look at the photo!'

'Yeah, so what?'

Of course, I'd forgotten that Callum hadn't seen any of the photofits or real pictures of Viola's dad, so he couldn't see what I saw. I had to explain.

'This Sir Alex King looks like Viola's dad. He's maybe a bit older, but he could easily be the man in the photofit pictures of the bank robber.'

'Aha,' said Callum. 'That's *very* likely – a millionaire who needs to rob a teeny weeny bank. All it proves is that photofits are unreliable.'

I could tell that he was still feeling miffed about my reaction to his ridiculous escape plot. But even so, I felt he was right and I could feel all my excitement draining away. 'And Mrs Armitage actually saw the criminal and identified him,'

I sighed. 'Oh Cal, it obviously was Viola's dad who did it.'

'You've changed your mind pretty quickly. Why do you say that?'

I didn't really want to tell him that my researches had made it painfully clear that Viola's dad was no stranger to crime, whatever Viola thought. But I knew I had to, so I said what I had found out about all the petty crimes as well.

'Do you think Viola knows about all that?' he asked.

'Maybe, maybe not. I don't want to be the one to tell her . . .'

I read the whole article about King later. He's moved into the vast mansion at the top of the hill and wants 'to put something back' into the community he grew up in. Doesn't really sound like a crook, to be honest. Maybe the Alex King thing is what detective writers call a 'red herring', i.e. something that just doesn't add up. I have just looked it up in *Brewer's Dictionary of Phrase and Fable*. NB: this is one of my own writer's tips: get one of these very good books and it will tell you loads about words. I learned that a red herring is a 'diversion which distracts from a line of enquiry'. And it comes from drawing a red herring (i.e. one that has been smoked and salted) across the path of a fox, so its scent is destroyed and hounds can't find it. All of the above is of course a red herring itself, distracting me – and you, Dear Reader – from getting on with my novel . . .

I wish I hadn't gone into the archives now, because I have found out loads of stuff I didn't want to know about Viola's dad. So now that I am in an agony of indecision, I must lose myself in *The Bat of the D'Urbervilles*.

The Bat of the D'Urbervilles (ctd)

In the shadowy spooky Baker Street basement, Sir Horatio read on from the stories of the D'Urberville curse.

'Of all the men who rode out the night that Vladimir died, all but one have perished. Two from strokes that very evening, four from madness brought on by these dreadful events. One alone kept his wits and related these dark deeds to me, the second Earl of D'Urberville. And I write them now in the hope that future generations may be saved from the fate that befell my father. Be not wicked, ye sons of D'Urberville, and ye shall come to no harm!'

As Sir Horatio laid down the script, his hand shook shakily and a few drops of sweat dripped on to the ancient parchment.

'Has anything else unusual occurred?' Holmes asked, as if such horrors were all in a day's work to her (which, of course, they were).

'Yes,' said the troubled fourteenth Earl of D'urberville. 'I have also been sent this.'

He then produced, from his waistcoat pocket, a crude sheet of paper on which were the words:

Do NoT gO To D'URbeRville hALL AS YoU vaLUe YouR LiFE.

'I see your messenger was reading yesterday's

Manchester Guardian,' said Holmes, with a twinkle in her bright blue eye, bringing an air of normality back into the hitherto hushed and haunted study. 'They have simply cut and pasted words from the leader column,' continued Holmes, playing a few strains of a melifluous melody on her beloved Stradivarius violin as the two men gazed at her in gratifying admiration. 'Exceptionally interesting, don't you agree, Watson?'

Well, I bet you are all very interested. But I'm not going to reveal the mystery to you yet, because I haven't worked it out . . .

Xerxes was licking my inky fingers as I closed *The Bat of the D'Urbervilles* with a sigh. I wonder if it's fishy ink? Maybe from an octopus?

Chapter Five

Dreamed all night about bats, and banks, and books, and belfries, and blame, and bananas . . . this alliteration thing can drive you bats. Or barmy. Or bonkers.

Part of me wanted to tell Viola everything I'd found out. But it was not good about her dad. He'd been in trouble lots of times before, and maybe she didn't know anything about that. Perhaps Aunt Laura was right, and I'm just going to cause problems by bringing it up. And how could Viola think I was really trying to help her and that I still wanted to be her friend if I just made her feel worse about her dad than she did before?

I did so much fretting about this that Candice, who is always in such a hurry in the mornings that she normally wouldn't notice if I sat down to breakfast with an axe sticking out of my head, asked me what was the matter.

'Nothing,' I told her.

'That's all right, then,' Candice said brightly. 'Must fly.'

'I might ask Viola back to tea,' I called after her.

'Fine,' I heard a distant voice say before the front door banged.

At school, I tried to corner Viola at break, but she was in a huddle with the banshees and ignored me. Jason Kramer, the school creep, had an arm around her, which she didn't seem to mind. I couldn't believe it.

But I did follow her to the loos at lunchtime and get her on her own. She was peering into the mirror and examining her eyes.

'Is that make-up?' I said from behind her. 'You're not supposed to wear that at school.'

She spun round, looking furious. 'You a teacher now?'

'I just don't want you to get in trouble,' I said, backing off.

'That's my choice,' Viola said. 'Sorry, I forgot, you don't leave people to get on with their own lives, do you?'

'Viola . . .' I began, but Gemma and Steph, two girls from Year Ten barged in, singing loudly. Steph went into a cubicle, Gemma examined a spot in the mirror, Viola and I went quiet.

'Eeeyuuuw,' Gemma moaned. 'It's gonna be bigger than me head soon.'

'Zap it,' came Steph's voice from the cubicle.

'I can't, me face'll look like a hole in the road,' Gemma said.

'Does anyway,' Steph said, cackling.

Gemma kicked the loo door open and took a picture with her mobile.

''Ere, lay off you pervert,' Steph said, still laughing.

'I'm going to send it to Graham,' Gemma squealed, fiddling with her phone.

Steph came out and tried to grab the phone. Then they saw us staring at them.

'What you looking at?' Gemma demanded.

'Nothing . . . we . . .' Viola began.

'Maybe I should send the picture to you two instead,' Gemma sneered. They laughed louder than ever and went out arm in arm.

Viola and I looked at each other.

'Sorry,' I said.

'Sorry,' she said.

And we went out arm in arm too.

'I don't want to be like that, you know,' Viola said as we crossed the playground. 'Like them. It isn't really me. Then sometimes I do. They make things seem simpler. I don't seem to know who I am at the moment. I wish this stuff with my dad had never happened.'

'There's something else I want to tell you about that,' I told her. 'Maybe it'll help us to find the answer.'

She looked doubtful.

'Don't worry, it's not another Callum escape plan. It's something I found in the paper. Come back to tea and I'll show you.'

And Viola looked really pleased.

When we got home, of course, I started with the hopeful bit and showed her the article about Sir Alex King.

'It's him! It's the robber! He looks really like Dad! We've solved it!' she screamed and flung her arms round me.

'I'm sorry Viola, but, the more I've thought about it, the more I don't think it can be him,' I said, trying to get her to face facts. 'Sir Alex King has made millions selling ships and things, not robbing banks.'

'What about the robber barons?' Viola retorted. 'Every crook has to start somewhere. Anyway the robbery was three years ago – he might not have been rich then . . .'

This was the first time it really sank in with me that Viola's dad had been behind bars for three whole years. Bugsy would have been only one and Viola eight.

'Oh. Viola. I know it's terrible, but . . . I discovered more about your dad. I didn't want to, but . . .'

I tailed off. Why was I getting us into this? Why does Viola ever need to know?

'I know what you're going to say, that he's been involved in other bad stuff,' said Viola. 'I know that.'

'You do?'

'Yeah, Mum told me. She was trying to stop me constantly thinking he's innocent.'

'How did you feel about that?' I asked. I was relieved that she knew, in a way.

'It didn't stop me believing in him.'

'Even though he'd done those other things?'

'He's always been good to me. But I can see why Mum feels let down. He's told her he's turning over a new leaf a few times, and then he doesn't. But he's always admitted the other stuff, and all of it was just really really little things. He says he had nothing to do with the robbery he's inside for now, and I believe him, I swear I do.'

Viola's eyes were blazing.

Obviously I didn't look convinced. 'I knew you wouldn't believe in him, if I told you all of it. Especially the gun bit. That's why I never told you,' she added. 'But I swear to you, Cordelia, that my dad would never risk hurting anyone else. Don't you see, that's how I know it wasn't him! If it had just been any old robbery, it might be different. But I just know Dad would never, ever use a gun!' She tailed off.

Looking at her face I so wanted her to be right. I imagined how I would feel if this was Howard. But then, teddy bear professors don't really do bank robberies. Wild kids like Fizzy Oakes, who start off bad, often end up worse . . .

On Saturday, Viola, Callum and I took the 72B bus to Stanford, to robbery witness Mrs Armitage's needlework shop. Viola had prepared herself well with three pictures: the original photofit; a picture of her dad; and the image of

Sir Alex King cut out of the *Falmer Gazette*.

The bus squeezed through tiny villages of ancient little houses I hadn't known existed – except maybe from a buggy when Howard and Candice used to go for drives into the country on Sunday lunchtimes when I was a baby. They hadn't done that for a long time. Stanford was a bit bigger, but the houses still looked like dolls' houses.

'Probably go mad in a place like this,' Callum said, looking around. 'Nothing to do.'

'I don't know,' I said. 'You could imagine you were living in another century. You could be a smuggler, or a highwayman, or . . .'

'Or a bank robber?' Viola said, gloomily.

'They didn't have banks in the old days,' Callum said.

'Where did you get money from then?' I asked him.

He thought for a bit. 'Dunno. Rich people just had castles and lands and haunches of venison and things, and kept treasure in jewel-encrusted chests guarded by mad axe murderers and ravening hounds. Nobody else had anything, they just worked for the rich people for a crust of bread, or the ravening hounds would be set on 'em. I s'pose you only need banks when everybody's got some money.'

'Look, there's the shop,' I said. A sign read 'Armitage's Sundries'.

'What are sundries?' Viola wondered.

'Day after Saturdays,' Callum said.

'Kind of pudding,' I contributed.

'That's sundaes,' said Viola.

'Well, anyway, it has to be the right shop. Let's go and see.'

It wasn't like any shop you can find on our high street. There was yellowing transparent paper behind the glass and lots of balls of wool and reels of cotton and bits of coloured cloth in the window. A little bell rang as we went in, and there was Mrs Armitage, standing behind the counter. She looked like someone out of a baby's bedtime book, with pink cheeks, neat grey hair, and a big welcoming smile.

At first, we pretended we were doing a local history project, as Callum said we shouldn't 'contaminate the witness's evidence by letting her know we were involved with the accused'.

Mrs A was bright as the rows of buttons lined up on her counter. She was over seventy now, she said, but she refused to retire 'until they carried her out'.

'I'd curl up and die if I had nothing to do, dears,' she said. 'I can still thread a needle without glasses. I'm always busy. I just came back from Alaska where my daughter took me on holiday last week.'

'Alaska?' we chorused. 'That's miles away. Isn't it very cold?'

'Well, I didn't walk it. And it's not cold if you wrap up warmly, dear. Very important to have new experiences when you get to my age. Gives you something to think about rather than just your aches and pains.'

Mrs Armitage said she could remember the robbery 'as if it were yesterday'. She gave us a vivid description of tripping the villain up and then whacking him on the head with her umbrella. Viola winced and I wondered if she was thinking that it might have been her dad after all.

'You whacked him on the head with your bumbershoot?" said Callum, without thinking.

Mrs Armitage let out a great bellow of laughter.

'Bumbershoot! I haven't heard that word since I was a girl back home in Washington DC! My grandma used to use it. Wherever did you hear that?'

'You mean it isn't English?' I asked. 'You don't think Sherlock Holmes would have used it?' I felt childishly disappointed. It was my favourite Victorian word.

'He might have, dearie, but it's an old American word.' Now she'd mentioned it, I could hear the faint twang of the American accent she must have had when she was a girl.

Viola was irritated. 'Mrs Armitage, you say you can remember the robbery as if it were yesterday? Do you remember the robber's face really clearly then?'

'I'll never forget it, dearie. You don't forget a man with a gun up this close, do you?'

Then Viola laid out the three pictures.

'Can you say which of these two men it was?' she asked.

Mrs Armitage looked flustered. She said a few things about it all happening so fast and her eyes not being what they used to be and then she blushed because she had just told us about the needle-threading. She paused for a moment.

'Do you know dear, these two men do look alike, don't

they? They both look like the photofit. I'll be honest with you and say it could have been either of them.'

Viola then poured out her story and Mrs Armitage looked most upset to think she might have caused a miscarriage of justice.

'Look dear, if you can find anything else to link this Sir Alex to the crime then I will do my best to help, of course. But we must be absolutely sure before we start spreading rumours. This is a respectable man, a pillar of the community, and a powerful man, too. You have to think hard before you start accusing somebody like that of a thing like this.'

We were in high spirits as we left poor Mrs A. I felt sure we were on the right track at last, but Callum remained unconvinced.

'We still need another CLUE – something that really links Sir Alex to the crime,' he said. 'A chance likeness isn't enough to convince the police to re-open the case. We'll have to get into King's mansion somehow. Maybe break in . . .'

'Not another of your fake-blood-and-knife schemes, please,' I said. 'And there must be other ways of finding out what goes on in there without us having to pretend we're Spiderman.'

I went back to the *Falmer Gazette* office and photocopied every reference to King that they had. Callum found lots of stories about him on the internet, including aerial photos of the mansion. Viola had found a whole feature about him and his house in *Hello!* magazine.

Our sleuthing revealed that King's place was vast: swimming pool, tennis courts, a purpose-built theatre . . .

'Ill-gotten gains,' I growled. 'Probably been a robber for years and just made up all that stuff about shipping.'

'Unlikely. I mean it's OK to think it could be him,' Callum said, as we pored over the aerial pictures of King's mansion. 'But if we can't get close to Sir Alex we can't confront him. His place has got more security than the Bank of England.'

'But this is interesting,' interrupted Viola, reading from the *Hello!* article. 'His dad was the gamekeeper on the mansion's estate. So he lived in the keeper's cottage there when he was a kid. Now he's bought the mansion for himself, he's going to rebuild the gamekeeper's cottage as a toy museum, with all the toys in it he was never able to have. Hmmm. That doesn't sound like a fiendish criminal mind at work.'

'But maybe he really grew up all bitter and twisted and full of envy because his dad was a servant,' Callum pondered. 'That's often how criminals start out.'

'Exactly,' said Viola. 'And now he wants to seem like Robin Hood, trying to make himself sound so good and great. Look, it says here that he wants to 'give something back' to the community. And so he is allowing the Easter Fair to take place in part of his grounds this year!'

When she said that we all had the same idea at once. The Easter Fair! A perfect opportunity!

'We can get in that way!'

But no. Viola read on. The Easter Fair was to be held in fields adjoining the house – separated from the gardens by a high wall . . .

'Pah!' said Viola.

As it happened, the more I thought about it all, the more I lost heart. 'Listen,' I said, reading from *Hello!*, 'he's been given awards and medals and tributes and stuff from just about everybody. And look at these pictures of all his boats. He seems to have made his fortune years ago. Why would he need to rob a bank?'

'Maybe he was bored,' Callum suggested. 'He had every-thing money could buy, except excitement.'

Viola looked downhearted.

I felt worried that we were raising Viola's hopes only to let her down again and that her refusal to face up to her dad's murky past might be blinding her to the obvious truth – that he did the robbery all along.

After another sleepless night, I emailed Aunt Laura about it. This is what she wrote back:

```
There are bad people in this world,
Cordy, and lots of them are somebody's
father. Try to help Viola come to terms
with it.
```

I supposed she was right. There must be hundreds of thou-sands of villains who have kids. Even murderers are probably nice to their own kids. Life is not as simple as I would like it to be sometimes. But I still couldn't let go of the idea that Viola's dad might be innocent. I kept thinking of how awful it would be to be in jail for something you hadn't done.

So I went on sifting through all the articles late into the night. And then I saw something that made my heart stop. Surely this was the extra clue we'd been looking for. It was a tiny paragraph at the bottom of page two of that day's *Falmer Gazette*.

Workmen Discover Gun in Demolished Cottage
Workmen demolishing the old gamekeeper's cottage in the grounds of millionaire Sir Alex King's Spiggott Hill mansion were surprised to discover a Berretta 92FS amid the rubble. Sir Alex expressed surprise and said he wasn't aware that gamekeepers ever used Berrettas and that in his grandfather's day they used rifles.

'Perhaps my grandfather had a secret life,' he joked. 'But on a more serious note, I'd like to put on the record that this gun has nothing whatsoever to do with me.'

Police have taken the gun away for forensic tests, and Sir Alex expressed the hope that it might be returned to form part of the Spiggott Hill Mansion Museum, which he is intending to open to the public next year.

I rummaged through my stacks of old papers to find the original report of the crime. YES! The police reports said that from the CCTV footage of the robbery they were almost certain the robber was carrying a Berretta 92FS!

It was two a.m. I emailed Callum. And fell into bed, my mind whirring. Surely this was the missing link?

Of course, innocent folk don't languish in jail in the world of Charlotte Holmes, who gets everything right – and that's why writing is so much fun. You can make everybody do exactly what you want, and they never complain about it. So I'll just fill you in on the next thrilling episode . . .

Laura Hunt's Top Tips for Budding Writers:
Try to get into a routine. Finding a regular time of day you can write is an excellent idea. Do about two hours, then free your mind with a walk, or a hot soak in a bubble bath.

Oh, great. What about people who have school? Or homework? Or friends? Or TV?

The Bat of the D'Urbervilles (ctd)

Dr Callum Watson was disturbed to discover that he was to travel with Sir Horatio to D'Urberville Hall, while Charlotte Holmes stayed behind in London.

'You cannot do this to me, Holmes,' Dr Watson protested piteously. 'In all our many adventures such as have enthralled the nation with their deeds of derring-do and creepily cliff-hanging calamities, we have always faced the Dark Forces of Doom as a Dauntlessly Daring Duo.'

'Trust me, Watson,' Charlotte Holmes chortled, cheerily chucking him under his chiselled chin. 'You are fearful because you are much stupider than me, and cannot see the wood for the trees. But I promise you, all will be well, and we will bring this bedevilling bat to book. Go with Sir Horatio, and send me regular reports on everything you see. Make sure you tell me everything about the neighbours in the nearby neighbourhood.'

Two days later, after reluctantly travelling to the dank dreary fog-bound moor and the ghastly, ancient, tottering pile of D'Urberville Hall with Sir Horatio, Dr Callum Watson sent Holmes his first report:

Dear Holmes,

I must confess I do not like it here. The house, a rambling place of infinite desolation and gloom, is filled with secret rooms, echoing passages and doomy dungeons. Everywhere you are followed by the eyes of countless spectral ancestors, watching you from the portraits in the dim corners of the vaulted rooms. A chill fog arises every evening from the moor, a dismal, dreary and desolate place indeed Holmes, not improved by the eerie fact that it harbours an insane criminal, one Abel Dark, who has staged a fantastic escape from Doom Valley prison with the aid of ropes, abseils, lock-picking, disguises and much more. Even now this desperado lurks somewhere in the darkness, waiting to tear our throats from our necks. As to the neighbours, thank the Lord there is a kindly naturalist, a Mr Bruce Wayne, and his charming sister, for whom, I fancy, Sir Horatio has conceived a passion, for we visited them for tea yesterday and his face lit up like a small child's when the dark beauty smiled at him.

Otherwise, it is a lonesome place, with only a smattering of ancient admirals and a yodelling yokel or two. The servants, I believe, know more than they are saying. The Burymores are a middle-aged couple who have been with the family some years, but the man has a cold eye and exceptionally long and fearsome teeth. He looks for all the world like a vampire, Holmes, which in the circumstances is unsettling. He creeps about the house at night and his wife is pale and seems always on the verge of tears. Is her husband tormenting her?

Does he hold some dark and dastardly secret that she has the power to unlock? I tell you, Holmes, I don't like the cut of his jib. And all the while the village gossips talk of glimpsing a giant bat . . . and, ludicrous though it is, I fancy I have heard the flapping of spectral wings myself. I fear Sir Horatio is in imminent danger, and I make sure that he never travels alone upon the moor.

I wish you were here with me and did not have to stay in London to solve the mysteries of the ailing infants of Aylesbury, the dastardly disappearance of demure damsels in Dunbar and the beastly burglary from the Barnstaple blood bank. I hope to God this gets to you Holmes, for I am sore afraid.

Your faithful friend, etc,

Dr Callum Watson

'A fantastic escape from prison . . . If only it could be like that,' I sighed, thinking of the challenge to come.

Chapter Six

'I'm sick of sitting in this tree,' Callum said.

'You never say that about your own tree,' I said, a bit huffily. 'Live a little. Broaden your horizons. Try a different tree once in a while.'

'Right,' came Viola's voice from the next branch. 'From here we can see all across the Shire, and into the land of Mordor . . .'

We were, of course, spying on Sir Alex's mansion. Even the gun in the cottage hadn't been enough to convince Callum that Sir Alex was the guilty party, so we were looking for more clues. Unfortunately, sitting in a fir tree overlooking the mansion's grounds for five whole days had not proved to be very exciting. At least we weren't freezing any more. It was February half-term, grey and clammy, and we were beginning to think we were wasting our young lives . . .

Callum was complaining that he would be expelled because of not doing his homework, and we hadn't seen a single suspicious thing – just a few ordinary-looking people coming in and out, and no sign of Sir Alex.

'It's not Mordor, after all,' grumbled Callum. 'It would be all right if we could see the occasional regiment of orcs, or a fire-breathing dragon lighting up the gloom, but all we can see is this boring bloke's tennis courts and swimming pool, and a perfectly innocent helipad. There isn't even a helicopter firing heat-seeking rockets at the exhausts of MI6 agents' cars.

'What's that noise, then?' Viola asked.

The rumble of a distant helicopter was plain to hear. Pretty soon it came into view. It was flying low, and began to hover over Sir Alex King's grounds. The helicopter was a definite improvement on nothing. Callum focused his dad's binoculars on it.

'Look,' hissed Callum.

A black people-carrier with darkened windows swept up to the helicopter landing pad, and a figure got out.

'That's him,' I said. 'That's Sir Alex King.'

'Arch-villain,' said Callum, in a dramatic voice.

The helicopter landed, and two men in black suits got out, carrying briefcases.

'Timers, plastic explosives, high-velocity rifles broken down into parts,' Callum marvelled.

Viola groaned. 'It's just two men with briefcases,' she said.

But they were certainly in a hurry. Crouching under the

helicopter's blades, they ran towards the black car. They quickly shook hands with Sir Alex and jumped in. The automatic iron gates opened as they approached and the car sped through on to the road into town.

'Get after them!' I shouted to Callum. 'Give me the binoculars, I'll talk you in!' We were really getting into this sleuth stuff now.

Callum and Viola scrambled down the tree and leaped on to the bicycles they'd hidden in the bushes. If they were quick they could still head off Sir Alex at the pass (sorry, that's the crossroads with the launderette on the corner). I watched through the binoculars as Callum and Viola hurtled off, arriving at the crossroads just a second or two behind Sir Alex's sinister-looking black car. I called Viola's mobile.

'He's on the road that leads straight to the High Street,' I told her.

With a sigh of relief, I could see the car had got stuck behind a dustcart, with Callum and Viola not far behind it. Then I lost them. I just had to hope the dustcart would hold them up until they got into town and Sir Alex might start doing something suspicious.

I sat in the tree for what seemed an age. Then my mobile rang. It was Viola.

'How's it going?' she said. Sometimes Viola has no sense of how people are supposed to talk in whodunnits and spy stories.

'I'm in the same tree you last saw me in,' I said. 'Not much else is going on apart from that. How's it going with you?'

'Great. He's parked outside the bank in Mule Street.'

'Cor, really? Has he put a stocking mask on?'

'Don't think so. They're all just sitting in the car. Wait a minute . . . something's happening. They're all getting out.'

'Are they going into the bank?' I asked, hardly able to believe it.

'No . . . they're . . . going down the alleyway next to the bank. They've disappeared. Ohmigod, the alarm's gone off!'

Even up the tree on the phone, I could hear the sound of the bank's burglar alarm.

'It's a robbery,' I shouted at Viola. 'Call the police! Dial 999!'

'Hang on, the alarm's stopped. They must have disabled it,' I could hear Callum shouting.

There was a long silence from Viola.

'What's happening, what's happening?' I squawked down the phone. A couple of rooks flapped out of the tree, cawing crossly at the disturbance.

'Nothing . . . no, here they come. They're coming out again. They're running to the car. They're driving off.'

Pretty soon I saw the black car coming up the road from town, back to Sir Alex's house. The car raced back into the grounds, the helicopter started up, the two men in suits shook hands with Sir Alex and got into it, and off it went.

My mobile rang.

'Coo,' came Viola's voice. 'That was exciting.'

'Did you call the police?' I asked her.

'Didn't need to. They were here in no time. They went into

the bank for a bit, and then went away again. I suppose we'll have to tell them it was Sir Alex and his men who did it, and we saw it all.'

'Or maybe not . . .' I said, slowly.

'What do you mean?'

'Well, if we blow this now, how are we going to prove your dad was innocent?' I asked. 'Just because Sir Alex might have committed a crime today, it doesn't prove he committed another three years ago. We have to confront him with that one, and then throw this in to nail him once and for all.'

It was past teatime for all of us, so we packed it in. I bet Sherlock Holmes didn't have to worry about mealtimes.

I spent the evening poring over the events of that afternoon. Sir Alex looked as if he was still up to his old tricks, multi-millionaire or not. Maybe Callum was right, and he did it for fun. But we still needed proof, the kind that would stand up in a court of law. We had to get into his house and find irrefutable evidence. But how?

Then school life unexpectedly offered a way in.

The next afternoon we were rehearsing the amazingly terrible *Maiden at the Mast*. Things have gone from bad to worse, I have to tell you. Or maybe that's from worse to worser.

There's scenery now, which has been made by the resistant materials tech class and the art classes together.

Resistant materials is about half right – the scenery's not resistant enough to stop falling over every five minutes, but it's certainly resistant enough to give you quite a nasty bang on the head when it does. This unfortunately happened to the smallest girl in my class, Alice Cooper (it's a pity she has the same name as the ultra-weird, Halloween-type old-school rock legend, because she looks as if she'd have trouble eating baby-food let alone babies), and she disappeared completely under a big triangular thing that was meant to represent a live volcano. She was so shocked she was a bit like a live volcano herself for a while.

Then there's the IT teacher, Mr Giggs's amazing computerised lights and sound effects. They've made the whole thing a lot more fun for us, but not for Miss Delaware, who has been tearing her hair out. Some pretty good flashing lights happened today, but the sound effects started off as a roots reggae radio station from somewhere in Jamaica, which admittedly had something to do with the Caribbean but not much to do with pirates (unless you count pirate radio), and then turned into a message from a minicab driver using very rude words while trying to order a takeaway pizza from someone who didn't speak English.

Mr Giggs had another go and this time got *The Archers* before he finally found the bit that makes weird alien noises. I thought Miss Delaware was going to cry louder than poor Alice Cooper at this stage, but when Tobylerone came out from behind a painted wooden 'wall' pretending to do his trousers up and she realised someone had added a TOILETS sign to it, everyone laughed so much she gave up and joined in.

'You're all HOPELESS,' she trilled. Mr Simpkins looked anxiously round from the piano to see if she was including him, but she smiled sweetly at him and we all went 'Aaaahhhhhhh'.

When order was restored, Miss Delaware and Mr Simpkins got us doing the grand finale. This is where all the pirates and aliens, apparently well dead after the last great battle, spring to their feet (or tentacles or peg-legs), brought back to life by The Power of Song. Everybody then links whatever bits of themselves they can to every other person, and we all do a kind of dancing crocodile around the scenery, waving our arms in the air.

The stage that's been put up at the end of the gym, however, wasn't built for this. None of the scenery was still standing after about a minute of the dance, except for the wall with the TOILETS sign on it. Several aliens fell off the back and ended up thrashing around behind the stage like overturned beetles. Mr Giggs's soundtrack started playing country and western music, which brought the grand finale to a confused halt. Tobylerone tried to rescue the situation by yelling something incomprehensible and drawing his pirate cutlass in a triumphant gesture – but caught Lucia DiMaggio (a beautiful but very hot-tempered person you definitely do not mess with) in the ear with it, and within a nanosecond the two rolled off the stage, struggling and scratching at Miss Delaware's feet.

And Viola, still tied to the mast because Eric Cubicle had forgotten to untie her in his haste to pitch into the Great Battle, burst loudly into tears. This was nothing new, so nobody took any notice. Poor Viola has been bursting into tears at the mast (and there is a real mast now, adapted by the resistant materials class from what looks like an old hat stand) all through the rehearsals. Maybe it's something to do with being tied up reminding her of her dad, also a helpless captive, in prison.

'STOP IT, STOP IT!' Miss Delaware yelled at everybody. Moaning at us all for 'not caring', she called off the rehearsal and sent everybody home.

But Viola was still crying, and even in the mood she was in, Miss Delaware was sympathetic. She even suggested that maybe Viola should see the school counsellor. Horrified at the thought of anyone else finding out her circumstances, Viola spluttered that she was just depressed that our wonderful musical was not going to find a wider audience.

'She's so keen to act, you see,' I added, but Miss Delaware didn't need any further persuading. Instead, she launched into her usual moan about the dreariness of the hall, the lamentable funding for the arts in schools, the fact that top universities didn't appreciate drama, the tragedy of her lonely quest and her longing for Falmer North to be a performing arts academy.

And that's when I got my Big Idea.

'I know where we could perform it instead!' I squeaked. 'Let's write to that new millionaire who's moved into the mansion on the hill! He's hosting the Easter Fair there and he's got his own theatre! Let's see if he'll let us put our musical on there, and maybe he'll give us some funding too, for being a performing arts thingy.'

Miss Delaware looked doubtful. 'But look at it,' she sighed. 'It's a disaster. We ought to draw a veil over it, not perform it for the whole county.'

'A few more rehearsals and it'll be fine,' I assured her. Miss Delaware looked excited for a moment. Then doubtful again. It was like watching the sun peeping in and out from behind clouds.

'I have heard Sir Alex wants to give something back to the community,' she said hesitantly.

'Exactly!' I said. 'He wants to give something back to the community, so let's write to him and tell him this is just the way to do it. Hundreds of people will see *The Maiden at the Mast*, not just boring old parents and teachers! It'll be great for the school. And with proper space and lighting and a curtain that works, just think how much better the show will be. Think what it will do for your reputation, Miss Delaware.'

I could see Miss Delaware imagining herself in the luxurious mansion. She had probably read last week's *Hello!* too, since no one from our town had ever been featured in it before. She was probably imagining that there would be all sorts of fabulous film stars swanning about, just as there were in the pages of *Hello!* and that they would spot her incredible talent as a director and Mr Simpkins's amazing talent as a writer, and ask them to make a West End version of *The Maiden at the Mast*, or – joy! – a Hollywood musical.

'Well, I suppose the worst he could do would be to say no,' she said. 'Why don't you draft a letter, Cordelia? But you must be sure to show it to me before you send it.'

Yipppeeee! Evil Sir Alex is bound to say yes, because he wants to seem like a goody. This will give me access to the mansion, and I will surely be able to nip upstairs to King's boudoir and riffle through his drawers in true detective fashion.

'Oh, sure,' said Callum, when I told him my plan. 'He's bound to have left his safe open, or have a drawer by his bed with all the reports of the crime circled in red, so his wife can see them. More likely he'll have a diary under his pillow with the whole thing confessed, or perhaps a whole room in his cellar, with a secret sliding door, devoted entirely to his crimes . . .'

'Shatter-hauling shirkster!' I bashed Callum on the head with *Hello*! 'You know it's our best chance, you idiot. Now help me write a suitably grovelling letter.'

I wrote to Sir Alex in my best copperplate handwriting that I have been practising to make me a better writer. I had the dictionary open and used it for every word. Callum meanwhile, drew pictures from key scenes of the show, although he couldn't believe some of them and kept stopping to double up, helpless with mirth.

'You mean the aliens have tentacles? Won't the audience

think they're octopuses?'

'We're working on it. I think the whole thing is only happening because Miss Delaware has the hots for Mr Simpkins.'

We both knew the *The Maiden at the Mast* was dreadful, but we tried to make it sound brilliant and droned on about how, if Sir Alex supported it, he would be nourishing budding young talent from the most deprived areas of the town. I was very impressed with Callum's final artwork, which showed Viola roped to the masthead with an alien on one side and Tobylerone on the other, parrot and all. And he had drawn a caption: WILL SHE SURVIVE?

I noticed he had taken particularly loving care drawing Viola.

'How DOES she get away?' asked Callum, interested despite himself.

'Wait and see,' I said, a mite grumpily.

Miss Delaware loved my letter and said she was going to add 'a little note of my own'.

Viola was all excited again, now that we really were going to get into Sir Alex's lair. She was now one hundred per cent sure who the criminal was: the Evil Capitalist at the top of the hill. And I was certain, too.

A week after we'd sent the letter, Miss Delaware burst into the drama lesson grinning like a row of Cheshire cats. 'Wonderful news. Sir Alex has agreed to let us perform *The*

Maiden at the Mast in his purpose-built theatre as a finale to the fair! We are very lucky and must grasp this opportunity to show Falmer North at its best. With any luck the Mayor will come. And who *knows* what talent spotters may be gathering around Sir Alex's pool . . .'

So now we are well and truly on the way. Not to Hollywood, as I'm afraid the Mayor and any odd film stars will be dying of laughter at our show. But we ARE on our way to unmasking the True Villain and freeing Viola's dad!

Callum is almost as excited about it as Viola and me. Arlington Oratory hasn't changed him much really – he'd still far rather have an adventure like this than spend hours working out the molecular structure of champagne, or whatever it is they study in posh schools.

'Something's weird, though,' he said to me one soaking evening as we huddled in the tree house. The rain was slanty and we were far from dry.

'What?' I asked, through chattering teeth.

'There's been nothing in the paper about that business with Sir Alex and his hit men and the bank.'

'Hmm, you're right,' I said. 'Must be some kind of cover-up. Maybe the bank manager was in on it. Never raised the alarm.'

'But the alarm went off. That would ring at the police station, wouldn't it?' Callum objected. 'And anyway, the police came, didn't they?'

'They're all in on it, then. It's like *Enemy of the State* or something. It's a web of lies and corruption, with Sir Alex the spider at the centre.'

Callum was silent for a while. 'Are you sure about all this?' he finally said.

'Look, we've got to help Viola, right?' I replied.

'Right.'

'There was a gun found at the gamekeeper's cottage, right?'

'Right.'

'It was the same model used in the Stanford bank robbery, right?'

'Right.'

'Sir Alex looks very like the photofit of the Stanford bank robber, right?'

'Right.'

'Where did we last see him behaving very suspiciously?'

'At a bank,' Callum admitted.

'Exactly. It all fits. And anyway . . .'

'What?'

'It's the best lead we've got. Now, do you want to hear a bit of my thrilling new Victorian whodunnit?'

Callum looked interested – he is still keen on my writing at least.

'Go on then,' he said.

So, wet and cold as I was, I did. And it went like this:

The Bat of the D'Urbervilles (ctd)

After reading Watson's agonised call for help, Holmes knew she must act swiftly. Tales of a giant bat had been told in Aylesbury, Dunbar and Barnstaple and all the clues pointed in one direction. She knew she must hide near D'Urberville Hall, in one of the conveniently located Stone Age dwellings that scattered the rugged gorse-covered moor. From there, she could spy out the lie of the land and find further clues that would enable her to draw the noose of justice tight around the murderous villain's neck.

Swiftly, she packed a small bag with provisions enough for a few days and took the first train to the Moor of Despair, which surrounded the tottering pile of D'Urberville Hall. She telegraphed Watson.

'Fear not. I come to help. Meet me in the Stone Age cottage on the Moor of Despair at noon. Be sure to come alone, no one else must know of my arrival.'

'Thank God you're here, Holmes,' said Watson, just eight hours later, as they sat huddled in the Stone Age dwelling place with the misty fog descending. 'But why cannot you stay at D'Urberville Hall, in comfort with us, between the cursed but comfy sheets of the ancient clan of D'Urberville?'

'I needs must keep my presence secret a while longer,' said Holmes. But as luck, or ill-luck, would have it, events moved more swiftly than Holmes had bargained for.

At that very moment, a shrill cry rent the stillness of the fog-laden moor; a cry of such horror that it curdled the very blood in Watson's veins and nearly curdled Holmes's, too. Worse, above the horrifying cry there rose a sound far more ominous: a slow, steady flapping, as of gigantic wings . . .

The duo of daring detectives leaped up as one, cracking

their sturdy skulls on the lowly Stone Age ceiling. Recovering immediately, the intrepid investigators invaded the morose moor, straining their eyes, for dark was fast approaching.

'It was over there!' shouted Holmes. Her heart was thudding furiously in her chest. Had she come too late and betrayed Sir Horatio, who was even now dead of terror, or something worse?

The speedy sleuths sped swiftly towards the vile sounds and found – alas! – the crumpled body of Sir Horatio, stark and twisted, his familiar top hat had fallen to cover his face, but there was no hope of life, for a stake had been driven clean through his heart!

Charlotte Holmes's blood uncurdled and froze.

'Alas, poor Horatio,' she whispered to herself, unconsciously misquoting the great bard Shakespeare, for even in her grief she was educated far beyond the normal boring female of her historical period. 'It is my first failure,' she murmured as she knelt beside the body in deep distress.

Watson, following the time-honoured traditions of his noble profession, clasped the lifeless wrist between his finger and thumb in a hopeless effort to find a pulse, as Holmes gently drew the crumpled hat from the agonised rictus of terror that had once been a living breathing human man.

'What ho, Watson!' cried Holmes, leaping up and dancing a jig and playing a quick merry tune on her faithful Stradivarius violin that never left her side, even in emergencies such as this.

'Holmes!' cried Watson, his simple face darkened with shock. 'This is no time for jigs.'

'Oh but it is, Watson, it is. This is not Sir Horatio at all, but instead it is the body of Abel Dark, the wicked escaped prisoner. I recognise him from the engraving that was published in *The Times*. The bat has struck the wrong victim and we still may be in with a chance.'

'But how did he come to be wearing Sir Horatio's clothes?' asked Watson.

'Because he is the son of Mr and Mrs Burymore, Sir Horatio's faithful servants. I deduced this as soon as you sent me news of his escape, for the newspaper reported his change of name. It was clear to me from your description of their furtive behaviour, that the Burymores were sending him clothes and food out on the moor. That is how he came to be wearing Sir Horatio's old clothes. And that is why the villainous bat has got the wrong man. A case of mistaken identity.'

'Good heavens, Holmes, your brilliance always astonishes me.'

And so it was. Holmes and Watson took the dreadful news of the convict's demise to D'Urberville Hall, where they found the amiable naturalist, Bruce Wayne, his beautiful sister and Sir Horatio deep in discussion.

The faithful servants, Mr and Mrs Burymore, wept and wailed and confessed all. 'But still, this unearthly bat has murdered our son, and soon it will be our master's turn,' they sobbed.

Sir Horatio paced about in alarm. Could it really be true that a giant bat was out to batter him?

'I do not think so,' said Holmes. 'I believe there might be a human agency at work.'

'You must come and dine with us tonight, Sir Horatio,' said Bruce Wayne. 'You will be quite safe there.'

'That would be lovely,' sighed Sir Horatio, casting a yearning look at Mr Wayne's brooding, dark and beautiful sister.

While everyone soothed their nerves with brandy, Holmes drew Watson into the grand hall and whispered to him fiercely.

'See that picture? Who does it remind you of?'

Watson gazed blankly at the ancient portrait of a cavalier with a plumed hat, long hair and fancy moustache.

'It must be a D'Urberville, I suppose . . .'

'Look!' said Holmes, and pouncing upon the portrait she crooked an arm around the face to blank out the hat and hair, and stretched a finger across the moustache.

The face of the amiable naturalist, Bruce Wayne, sprang out of the canvas!

'Good God, Holmes,' said Dr Watson. 'Bruce Wayne is a D'Urberville!'

'Elementary,' said Charlotte. 'He's trying to grab the family fortune by killing his relatives.'

'But Sir Horatio is to dine there tonight,' Watson expostulated. 'You can't let him go there at night by himself.'

'All will be well this time, Watson,' Charlotte Holmes said. 'If my plan goes to plan, we will solve this mystery 'ere the clock strikes midnight. Or more likely, a few seconds after. I'll stake my life on it . . . if you'll forgive the expression.'

And so saying, Holmes told Watson of her daring plan to lay the ghost of the curse of the D'Urbervilles to rest forever more . . .

'Brilliant, Girl Writer,' said Callum. 'Let's hope life will imitate art . . .'

Laura Hunt's Top Tips for Budding Writers:
Plan your book. Have a brief outline of each chapter. Work towards your climax.

This is like those horrible SATs tests we had in Year Six. I thought writing was meant to be fun . . . Help! Later on, she says:

Don't always plan, try starting with something that interests you and see where you go.

Confused? It's all getting a bit like that gardening programme, where all those bonkers people with names like Bill Hopsack and Amaryllis Nettle disagree about how to pot a beansprout.

Chapter Seven

Laura Hunt's Top Tips for Budding Writers:
Don't introduce too many characters –
your reader may lose track of them.
Stick to just three or four.

*Help! I've already got Holmes, Watson and Sir Horatio
D'Urberville. Then, if you're reading this very book that you
are holding now, there's me, and Callum and Viola and
Xerxes, and Tobylerone and Miss Delaware and . . . Are you
losing track? Eeeek!*

The problem now, was what to do when we got into the mansion. Callum had convinced me that snooping around was hardly likely to turn up any clues about a three-year-old robbery. We needed some way to confront King and make him confess. But how?

Once again, we got the answer in the tree house. I can't think how we gave it up for so long, thinking it was babyish. It's ended up being the bestest place to have ideas, just like it was when we were little.

'It's nearly March. The Easter Fair's in four weeks' time. And every day that passes is like a year for Viola's dad,' I said. 'We have to have a *plan*!'

'Have you heard of Hamlet?' Callum asked, as if it meant something.

''Course I have,' I said. 'He's one of those people in Shakespeare who keeps getting poisoned and stabbed because he talks in poems and everybody gets well annoyed. What are you driving at?'

'Our English teacher was talking about him today,' Callum went on. 'She thinks the play about him is the greatest drama ever written. He's all miserable about his dad, the king, dying in mysterious circumstances, and how his horrible uncle, Claudius, had married his mum about five minutes later, and become king himself.'

'OK. So this Claudius obviously did it,' I said.

'Right. But how to get him to admit it?' Callum asked, staring very hard at me with his eyebrows up, and nodding.

'Wait a minute. Are you telling me all this not just to show me what a clever arty school your stinky-rich parents send you to?'

'Verily, the old-school penny finally droppeth.'

'OK,' I said, getting interested, 'what did Hamlet do?'

'He invited a group of actors to perform a play in his castle. And then he wrote a speech all about a wicked murder and got the actors to add it to the play – which his uncle was going to be watching! Then Hamlet saw Claudius turn pale and horrified and stuff, and knew he was guilty.'

'It wouldn't stand up in a court of law,' I said. That's a very important line for famous writers of crime thrillers to know.

'Well, they didn't have courts of law in Shakespearean days. They'd stab people as soon as look at them just for dissing their mums or something, let alone poisoning their dads. Anyway, Hamlet said: *The play's the thing with which to catch the conscience of the king*! It's one of the most famous lines ever written.'

'Of course!' I said. 'That's what we'll do with *The Maiden at the Mast*.

'Trouble is,' Callum pondered, obviously having second thoughts, 'you can't get Miss Delboy and Mr Simper, or whatever they're called, to write this bit, can you? That's what Hamlet did. He put in a speech about a murder to trap Claudius.'

'I know – we can't get them to rewrite it, but I can write a speech myself, and INSERT it. And the fact that he's called Sir Alex King – "Catch the conscience of the king". Surely that's a sign, isn't it?' I said.

'No,' said Callum. 'It's a coincidence, you puckering prater. Anyway, I can't quite see, even with your amazing talent, Girl Writer, how you are going to link a high street bank robbery with pirates. Or aliens. But I'll have a big think about it . . .'

While he did that, I spent the next few days baiting the trap. A chat with PC Budakli outside school turned up the news that he was going to be at the fair, running a community-policing stall under the slogan 'May the Force be with You and May You be with the Force'. I told him we'd all love him to see our play, since he'd almost become a Falmer North mascot. He said he could get someone else to look after the stall for a bit, and he'd definitely come.

So the Law was going to be present when we exposed the villainous Sir Alex. But I also needed Mrs Armitage, the crucial witness against Viola's dad. I found Armitage Sundries in the phone book, and called her up to explain.

'To be absolutely honest, dearie,' came Mrs Armitage's cosy voice on the phone, 'I didn't like to say this in front of your friend, it being her father and so on. But I do think it's extremely unlikely that a millionaire would want to rob our bank, don't you? But of course I'll come. I'd love to see Falmer North's musical. And to help out if I can.'

Ha! The trap is baited! The truth will out!

'The musical's the thing with which to catch the conscience of the King!'

My brilliant intervention in the play is proving much more difficult than I'd thought. This is truly the hardest task a Girl Writer has ever had. Callum and Viola are stumped, too. Firstly, I will obviously have to say the speech myself, which is not a problem Hamlet had. Secondly, I will be dressed in lime-green tentacles. Thirdly, I just can't see how I can realistically accuse a pirate, or an alien, or a maiden, all of whom are tossing about on the ocean waves, with doing a bank robbery. Callum was right.

Writer's block! It's not a big building full of writers, it's a thing you get when you can't think of what to write next! The only thing to do at a time like this is fall back on the faithful, and very successful, Aunt Laura.

Dear Aunt Laura,

In my detective book I am writing, I have come up against a problem and although I have been reading your writer's tips, there is nothing that tells me how to do what I want to do. It is a complicated plot thingy. I am trying to do what Hamlet did, and show the guilty person up by inserting a speech into a play. Unfortunately, I've already written loads and the play is a musical, about pirates and space aliens, and the criminal I want to unmask has done a bank robbery, so it's a bit hard to match them up. Have you got any tips? Please do not tell me to change the play to something else, or the crime, because it would mean rewriting the whole thing. I'd be incredibly, enormously grateful if you could email me back as I know you are so brilliant at complicated plots.

I saw an article about a vegan cat the other day! So I am attaching it in

case you can persuade Joan and Joan it
would be a good idea. Then they might
stop slaughtering so many birds. Candice
told me Bee Two ate a wasp! It is lucky
he is not allergic. Maybe it would be
good for the Three Bees if they were
vegetarian, too?

   Tons of love,

Cordelia xx xx

I had to wait three hours that evening for Aunt Laura's reply. But when it came, it was not at all encouraging.

Darling Cordy,

What a marvellous idea! I do approve of
your using a play to trap a villain!!
Splendid! I've always thought 'the play
within the play' (as it's called in
Hamlet) is a marvellous device!! But I'm
afraid I'm going to have to tell you
something rather honest. If a plot idea,
or a relationship, in your book isn't
working, you do sometimes have to bid it
goodbye, just as you do in your Real
Life (and as you will soon discover when
you have boyfriends!!!!). I know it's
awfully hard, darling, especially when
you have probably been counting your

words and pages and feeling proud of
your achievement, but that's how it is.
I have abandoned more plots and
characters than I can begin to count and
I always like to think of them living in
the land of 'the books that might have
been'. I hope they are all happy there,
especially Little Tinker, who was the
youngest child in *Mad Bad Dad* and who
had to be 'killed off'. It's awfully
hard for authors, almost like losing a
real friend sometimes. Sorry to ramble
on, but you have a choice. Either you
drop the 'play within the play' idea, or
you change the crime, or you change the
'pirates and aliens' musical. That does
sound fun! In fact, I think Howard told
me you were doing something similar at
school? Do let me know if so, I'd love
to come, as long as I'm not babysitting
the Three Bees. It's an age since I made
it down to London. It's a good idea to
base things in your story on real life,
of course, but you can make changes, you
know. Don't be afraid! It's all good
experience!!

Bertie did not swallow a wasp, but a
BEE. Terrifying, and awfully sad, as it

was one of those lovely big fat bumbles.
All three Bees now keep singing, 'There
was an old lady who swallowed a bee'. It
is rather trying. I have ordered one tin
of vegan cat food for Joan and Joan but
I don't hold out much hope.

Oooooooooodles of love,

L xxxxxxxxxxxxxxxxxxxxxxxxxxxxxxxxxxxx
xxxxxxxxxxxxxxxxxxxxxxxxxxxxxxxxxxxx

Well, I can't change the play, or the crime, because this is real life, not a book. And I think Aunt Laura has guessed that . . .

I emailed back saying the play was rubbish but I'd love her to come to something better later. Meanwhile, Plan B was forming in my overcrowded brain.

I consulted Callum and Viola, showing them what I'd decided to do.

'Well, it'll certainly do the trick if he's guilty,' said Callum.

'And if he's not . . . oh, I won't even think about that,' I said. But I did think about it, of course.

In order not to worry too much, I spent the next few days feverishly writing *The Bat*. It went rather well, though I say it myself, as things sometimes do when you stop caring so much. I wish there was another writing competition this term that I could enter it for.

Callum and Viola were not convinced by my Plan B, which involved confronting Sir Alex pretty directly. But they agreed it was our best hope and we all spent the last few evenings that weren't taken up with rehearsals before the fair making a prop that would look suitably like an alien message from outer space.

And now it is the fair tomorrow.

I can't believe that in just twenty-four hours' time we will have unmasked Sir Alex and set Viola's dad on the road to freedom . . .

I kept waking up and fingering the alien message that I'd folded under my pillow. In the still, dark night, it didn't seem it could work and it didn't feel much better the next morning.

Candice couldn't understand why I was so nervous at breakfast.

'You're only in the alien chorus, darling. It doesn't matter if you forget the words, there'll be plenty of others to carry on.'

Even now, I could still hear that little quivering note of disappointment in her voice that I wasn't playing the alien chief. Or the pirate chief. Or the maiden at the mast.

'You'll be fine as long as you don't trip over your tentacles,' Howard chuckled. 'I can't wait to see it.'

I'd tried every way I could think of to prevent them from coming, but who can stop their parents seeing their offspring perform? I would just have to go through with it and pray I didn't catch their eye as I confronted the villain, King. But now, as I was trying to eat some breakfast to give me strength for the day, I had to put up with one of Candice's spates of worrying. She suggested going through my whole part (four words) and the six choruses I was supposed to sing. I lied that there was an early run-through before the final run-through, and abandoned her in mid-worry.

My last words to her as I fled were, 'DON'T sit in the front three rows.'

I went straight round to Callum's. He was pacing about nervously.

'There's no point just sitting here sweating,' he said. 'We might as well go and try to enjoy the fair . . .'

'Suppose King didn't do it and I shame him in front of everyone? Will I get expelled?' I said, as we headed towards the grounds of King's mansion.

'Probably,' said Callum. 'I wish I was in the play, then I could do it. But really, you know, it ought to be Viola. It's her dad.'

'Impossible, when she's strapped to a mast. Anyway, she'd mess it up – you know she would. She's much too shy.'

'How come she's so good at acting then?'

'Oh, Miss Delaware says actors are often shy. She says they blossom on stage because they're pretending to be someone else who isn't shy. Anyway, Viola only has to be tied up and look miserable, you know. And she's excellent at that. She was only chosen for having long fair hair and a sweet face,' I added meanly.

'Very true,' said Callum dreamily. Then he blushed scarlet, for as we turned into the gates of King's mansion, there was Viola waiting for us, looking pale and shaky.

'I don't know what's worse,' she said, 'starring as the maiden at the mast or waiting to see if King did the deed.'

She hadn't heard us, obviously.

'Are YOU feeling OK, Girl Writer?' Callum asked quickly.

Me? I was shaking in my boots.

'Oh yeah, fine, it'll all go in my next great novel,' I assured him.

The meadows surrounding the mansion were packed with all the fun of the fair. Toddlers were drowning each other trying to bob for apples, shooting each other with bows and arrows and braining each other with coconuts. A bunch of grumpy-looking ponies were being forced to give yet more toddlers rides and a bunch of even grumpier clowns were making unrecognisable creatures out of balloons.

'What is the point of them?' said Callum. 'Whatever they make, it always looks like a dachshund.'

'Callum, you are losing the joys of youth,' I warned him. 'Let's ring a duck.'

Joy of joys, I won a purple furry toy telephone.

'This'll be great for Bugsy's next tea party with the Queen,' I said to Viola, and Callum looked at us as though we had finally completely lost it.

The three of us spent the next hour winning toys for Bugsy's tea party. Just as I was winning a pink velcro badger (which I don't think is very good for infants' natural history knowledge), I spotted Sir Alex King.

He was strolling around, twirling his moustaches like the Lord of the manor (which I suppose he is), with a pretty young woman and two little girls with him. They had on party frocks and sashes and bows in their hair. I gulped.

'Are those his, do you think?'

'Yes. He's got twins and a baby,' said Viola, who had obviously been paying more attention to the King family in her research than I had.

Suddenly Sir Alex seemed like a real person – somebody's dad. It made me feel queasy.

'I'm not sure I can go through with this,' I said.

'You've got to. Just because he's got kids doesn't mean he's a nice guy,' said Callum.

I knew that was perfectly reasonable, but it didn't help.

'So,' I asked Viola, 'does he look like your dad, now you see him in the flesh?'

'Yes, there is a similarity. I can see why Mrs Armitage confused them.'

If she confused them, I thought to myself. At that moment, Miss Delaware called us all to the run-through.

Compared to most of the rehearsals we'd done, the run-through wasn't too bad. Nobody fell over, nobody stood on anybody's tentacles, Tobylerone didn't pretend to be having a wee, and everybody even started and stopped in more or less the same place in the final song. Miss Delaware and Mr Simpkins beamed, waving us all off and duetting the show's greatest hits. Callum had watched the run-through with total disbelief, and the Delaware/Simpkins sing-song almost did for him.

'What a marvellous show, I wish we had such good drama teachers at Arlington Oratory,' he said to Miss Delaware, who went even pinker than usual. He waffled on a bit saying he wished she and Mr Simpkins could give their teachers some tips, and a grateful Miss Delaware almost cornered him into passing over their email addresses there and then.

'It's great to see people who love their work,' he said to me, trying to control his hysterics, after Miss Delaware had fluttered off pinkly. 'But it's obvious you can't wait till the end before you confront Sir Alex.'

'What do you mean?' I asked, anxiously.

'Well, the show's rubbish, isn't it? No offence. Your villain might think he's done his bit by seeing the first half, and bunk off for the second. You'll have to say your piece at the end of the first act.'

'Good call,' I agreed. 'But what's going to stop The Pink One from putting her oar in? I told her I'd do it at the end. She thinks it's a big thank you to Sir Alex from all of us for his generosity . . .'

'Well, now Miss Delaware and I are such good friends,' Callum winked, 'I'm going to stick close to her, and when you make your move I'll tell her you must have got muddled and nervous but that, never mind, you're still going to thank him and it'll look better not to interrupt. It is the interval after all – it's not like you're interrupting the whole show. It'll be fine.'

'I don't know if she'll buy that,' I said.

Callum shrugged. 'Fortune favours the brave,' he said. 'We can't run the risk of him bunking off after the interval. Let's hope for the best.'

We sneaked off with Viola to check my prop for the millionth time. I unrolled my scroll of beautifully prepared lime-green alien parchment, tied with an elegant fluorescent ribbon.

'Nice touch,' said Viola. 'He'll think it's an award.'

On the parchment we'd stuck the big newspaper story of the bank robbery and an enormous copy of the photo-fit of the robber. Underneath the photo-fit, in block capitals, were the words: SIR ALEX KING.

'Well, if that doesn't shame him, nothing will,' said Callum.

'But suppose he *didn't* do it?' I asked.

'You're not backing out?' The look on Viola's face as she spoke told me I just had to go through with it. An innocent man's freedom was at stake.

We decided to forget the awesome challenge ahead and enjoy the afternoon as much as we could.

Meanwhile, just to keep you in suspense, here's the latest:

The Bat of the D'Urbervilles (ctd)

After giving Sir Horatio strict instructions to leave Bruce Wayne's cottage at four minutes to midnight and to stay on the path, Charlotte Holmes and Dr Callum Watson followed him across the moor and took their positions a hundred yards from the evil naturalist's cottage.

At eleven-thirty, a deadly fog descended.

'Curses,' said Holmes, as the mists swirled around them, threatening to obscure the little house from view. 'This fog could undo all our plans.'

Tensely, they waited as the minutes ticked torpidly by.

Finally, they heard the sounds of people saying goodnight, the slam of a door in the dark, and the crunch of Sir Horatio's shoes on the path. Sir Horatio passed them in the fog, looking anxiously this way and that.

'Follow him, Watson!' Charlotte Holmes hissed heatedly. 'We mustn't lose him in this fog!'

The fog clung clammily to their clothes and wandered wetly into their wellingtons, as they faltered frantically over the rugged rocks to keep Sir Horatio in view. Then they heard a horrendously horrifying noise, of beating wings and squeaky squeals. They turned a corner just as Sir Horatio was crossing a clearing. He had heard the noise too, and stopped, peering aghast into the fuming fog.

Then they beheld a sight so unsettling that Holmes stopped dead in her tracks, for even she had been unprepared for a spectacle of such horror. Accompanied by a shrill, high-pitched whistling sound, an unearthly screeching cackle and a roaring rushing of wings, a giant bat, its eyes glowing, its wings flickering with green fire, its teeth dripping red as the daring detectives turned on their torches, plummeted through the air and fell on to Sir Horatio, thrusting him to the ground. Charlotte Holmes and Dr Watson stumbled across the rocks towards the flailing figures, Sir Horatio yelling in utmost terror. The giant bat looked up snarling at his unexpected assailants, then disappeared into the fog.

'What was it, Holmes, what was it?' panted Dr Callum Watson, helping the terrified toff to his feet.

'It was human, whatever it was,' Charlotte Holmes said, pointing her torch on to the path. Footmarks of a size ten Doc Martens showed in the mud where the giant bat had made its escape. Holmes also pointed above them, to where a steel cable had been stretched across the path from one rocky crag to another.

'A flying fox,' Holmes gritted gravely. 'Or, should I say, flying bat. This is where Bruce Wayne laid his dastardly trap, descending on that wire, wearing giant fake wings covered with luminous paint. Even though on this occasion he did not wear his bat-shaped boots that he wore to slay Horatio's uncle, his disguise was still so terrifying that anyone not as clever as me would have assumed they were being attacked by a spectral species.'

Laura Hunt's Top Tips for Budding Writers:
Revise, revise revise! Make sure you thoroughly exorcise, expunge and eradicate any boring or turgid or tedious or uninteresting or dull words that just take up acres and oceans of paper rather than move the story along at a spanking, rollicking, dynamic, speedy pace.

Hah! Obviously she should have written: 'Take out any boring words that fill space rather than move the story along.'

Chapter Eight

At the fair I won a mad-looking toy rabbit by ringing a plastic duck first time (Mr Simpkins had been trying to win it for Miss Delaware and looked miserably at me, so I gave it to him), Callum figured out how the airguns in the shooting gallery were bent to miss everything and ended up winning a bottle of whisky, which the stall-man wouldn't give him until Mrs Armitage pretended she was his aunt, and we all watched the trained-poodles dance show with poodles dressed in tutus leaping at the trainers' bottoms, to encouraging cheers from the crowd.

Then came the time to dress up for the actual performance of the dreaded *Maiden at the Mast*, and it suddenly dawned on us all how embarrassing it was going to be to flap around in stupid alien costumes in front of half the town.

'This is all your fault, Cordelia,' Jolene hissed at me, trying to tuck her mobile inside her alien suit. 'We could have just done this in the gym for our parents – now the whole world's going to see it.'

I ignored her, because I was doing this for a Higher Cause and soon they would all know that. We ran on stage to Mr Simpkins's jangling piano music, and I could see Bugsy jumping up and down in the front row. She had said she would be bringing the Queen, so that it would be a royal gala performance, and sure enough, she was waving the teapot over her head. She tried to run on to the stage with us, but Viola's mum grabbed her just in time.

Sir Alex was seated regally in the middle of the second row with his wife and daughters. His wife was clutching a little bundle, which I presumed was the baby. I got cold tentacles. Suddenly this seemed like a mad thing to do. And I was going to humiliate him in front of his children. Maybe they'd grow up really weird on account of it. But there seemed to be no way out now.

We lurched into the play and, as usual, pirates clattered around the stage shouting incomprehensibly, unidentifiable animals roared, and aliens fluttered about, squelching.

My big moment was approaching – it was the dramatic part just before the interval when the alien chief has captured Viola and the aliens are bent on world domination. We all formed a chorus line and wobbled forward singing Mr Simpkins's alien chorus.

'Think of Bill Sykes as a Dalek,' Mr Simpkins had told us.

Ex-term-in-ate, ex-term-in-ate,
We'll dom-in-ate,
You're all dead mate,
Woo woo woo.

As we neared the footlights I sprang forward, whisked off my bulbous lime-green head, smiled my brightest smile straight at Sir Alex and curtsied, swishing my tentacles. The audience went, 'Aaaaaaaaaaaaaaaaah', and Sir Alex beamed. Out of the corner of my eye I could see Callum holding Miss Delaware's arm and whispering feverishly to her, but it didn't look like it was working. I thought I'd better hurry things up.

'VerilyLordLeaderSireYourMajestyMrKing,' I gabbled and croaked at the same time.

Some of this noble speech was lost in gales of laughter because Bugsy, in the front row, had broken free of Viola's mum and was pulling one of my tentacles as hard as she could. This set off the Heartless Villain's younger daughter, who began pulling another in the opposite direction. I must have looked like an eight-legged pair of green jeans flapping on a washing line.

I could see Miss Delaware break free of Callum and advance towards me.

'I bring thou a message from another universe, a cosmos where goodness is rewarded and where evil is punished by a deadly doom,' I shouted, as fast and loud as I could over the din, and I threw my beautifully prepared rolled-up parchment into Sir Alex's lap.

Smiling even more broadly, he slowly unfurled it.

I have seen smiles vanish fast, but not that quick.

Sir Alex's mouth dropped open, and his brow clouded just like a villain in a book. His wife grabbed his arm, staring at the picture.

The baby howled as Lady King jumped up and almost dropped it. With her free hand, she yanked at her tentacle-clutching daughter, who suddenly let go – leaving only Bugsy, pulling as hard as she could, on the other end. With a ripping sound, the hated alien suit tore apart in two directions, one half tripping the approaching Miss Delaware, the other narrowly missing Viola's mum and Bugsy and then enveloping the Mayor in the front row. Tobylerone drew his sword, as he usually did in emergencies, and once again accidentally hit Lucia DiMaggio with it, resulting in the same free-style combat as last time, to scattered cheers from the crowd.

Sir Alex and Lady King stormed out of the hall dragging their weeping children, leaving me standing there in a T-shirt and shorts in a crowd of green aliens and tatty pirates, the audience laughing, shouting and jeering. I wanted a hole to swallow me up. Mr Simpkins, a crazed smile on his face, started playing – for some reason – the theme from *The Flintstones*. Callum, very fast off the mark I must admit, grabbed the big cardboard sign saying *Twenty-Minute Interval* and held it up.

Some left, some stayed, as if they couldn't take their eyes off the horrible events on stage. Scrambling to her feet, Miss

Delaware (who had now gone purple rather than pink) started yelling at me, obviously not caring any more who was listening.

I was vaguely aware of Callum, Mrs Armitage, Viola's mum and Bugsy all milling about on stage around me, and Viola, dragging the hatstand/mast behind her, trying to get to us.

'What do you mean by it, Cordelia Arbuthnott?' Miss Delaware screamed. 'You've ruined the performance!'

'Sir Alex is a crook!' I squeaked.

'He did the bank job my dad's in prison for!' cried Viola.

Miss Delaware was in no mood to listen. I looked round wildly for an escape route, but the only exit was blocked by – horrors! – a worried-looking Howard and a hysterical-looking Candice.

'Darling! What have you done?' shrieked Candice.

'I can explain it all,' I stuttered.

'Your daughter has behaved unforgivably,' interrupted Miss Delaware. 'Whatever was written on that piece of paper has given terrible offence to the one man who was likely to help our cause!'

She turned to us. 'You must apologise to Sir Alex this instant!'

'Never!' I said.

'I think you'd better,' said a voice from behind Eric Cubicle, who was nobly trying to untie the struggling Viola. He must have thought the best thing to do in this situation was at least carry out his own duties, even if nobody else was attending to theirs. 'Otherwise I'll have to nick you for disturbing the peace.' PC Budakli winked at Miss Delaware.

'But he's the robber! He's the man you thought was Fizzy Oakes!' I said.

'And Fizzy Oakes is my dad,' said Viola.

The crowd of pirates and aliens that had gathered round us fell back, except for Tobylerone, who hopped forward and put his hand on Viola's shoulder. Viola smiled gratefully.

'And it must be true, because otherwise Sir Alex wouldn't have stormed out, he'd just have laughed,' said Callum.

PC Budakli looked from me to Viola and back to me. He realised that we believed what we were saying, but that didn't make him believe it.

'Listen,' he said seriously. 'Sir Alex King didn't get rich by robbing a piggy-bank like the one on Stanford High Street. He had more money than I'll ever see years ago, and he made it by his own hard work. Anyway, when rich men commit crimes, they don't run about in stocking masks with guns.'

'But he did! He robbed the bank in Mule Street last Thursday! We saw him do it!' I spluttered. 'The alarm even went off!'

PC Budakli looked bemused, then the penny dropped. And he laughed.

'You have been busy, haven't you?' he chuckled. 'I went to check that out and the alarm had gone off by accident, because it was outside normal opening hours. The manager had done it himself – he was a bit embarrassed. Shows you even bankers are human.'

'But what about the two heavies with Sir Alex?' Callum insisted. 'The ones who came in the helicopter, in shades and dark suits.'

'Does that mean they're from the Mafia?' The policeman smiled. 'They were a couple of business associates of Sir Alex's. They'd all turned up to sign the papers for some property deal.'

Viola was staring at her feet. So was I. Callum kicked a barrel of rum. We all knew we'd made a dreadful mistake. I cursed myself. Charlotte Holmes would have done her research a lot better than this, I thought.

While Mr Simpkins made an announcement to the bemused audience that the second half would be a little delayed, PC Budakli and Miss Delaware marched us off in search of Sir Alex King.

'We may yet be able to save the day, if we explain ourselves,' trilled Miss Delaware. 'If you own up to your stupidity, that is, and apologise handsomely.'

She whispered in the ear of a man dressed as an old-fashioned butler, who whispered in the ear of a woman dressed as an old-fashioned housemaid. For a moment, I thought they were actors hovering in the wings before performing some other show, but in fact they were dressed that way because that's who they were: Sir Alex's very own maid and butler. The two of them whispered to each other a little more and then the maid scuttled off. She returned to beckon us and we were ushered down a long corridor and into a vast living room with oceans of polished floor and gigantic white leather sofas that I recognised from the article in Hello!'

Sir Alex sat slumped on a sofa in earnest discussion with his wife, who instead of looking sympathetic, looked furious.

PC Budakli gently pushed me and Viola and Callum into the centre of the room.

'Pardon me, sir,' he said to the millionaire. 'These children owe you an apology for what happened just now.'

There was a silence, and then Sir Alex said. 'Not sure they do, officer. It might be the other way round.'

'Go on, get it off your chest,' Sir Alex's wife snapped, tight-lipped. 'I don't want anything more to do with it.' She stormed out.

Sir Alex rang for tea, brought in by the maid. He sighed deeply and patted the sofa beside him. It was an invitation to sit down.

'Don't!' hissed Viola. 'He's obviously guilty.'

Sir Alex smiled a wan smile.

He looked directly at me and his piercing blue eyes were sad. 'She's right,' he said. 'I am guilty. Not of the bank robbery, no. I am sorry to disappoint you about that. But I am guilty of evasion. Of trying to keep unsavoury facts from the public eye. Of trying to preserve the privacy of those I love. And, yes, perhaps, of abandoning those I should have cared for . . .'

'What's he talking about?' Callum whispered in my ear.

I shrugged.

PC Budakli tapped me on the shoulder and said, 'Pay attention.'

Sir Alex smiled at us, and in a way it looked like a nice smile. 'I'll take it from the top, but I'd feel better if you sat down,' he said to us. 'I'm going to tell you a secret hardly anyone knows, and it's not easy to find the right words.'

Viola and I edged on to the blinding-white sofa. PC Budakli and Callum stood behind, the PC looking a bit uncomfortable in this swanky room. Mrs Armitage, Miss Delaware, Howard, Candice, Viola's mum and Bugsy all found seats (the room seemed to have about a million of them) opposite us. Sir Alex opened a big old photo album and passed it over for me and Viola to spread out on our laps.

'Look at the picture on the right,' he said.

It was obviously a picture of him, taken a long time ago. And standing next to Sir Alex was – Sir Alex!

Er . . . hello?

Viola and I looked up at him, wide-eyed, and I could sense Callum behind us doing the same.

'That's my brother Giles,' he said. 'My TWIN brother, Giles.'

The old penny beginneth to drop, I could imagine Callum thinking. I caught Viola's eye. The same obviously went for her.

'Giles and I both started out from the same place, but life turned out differently for him,' Sir Alex said. 'We grew up in these parts, our grandad worked till he dropped dead here in these very grounds and our dad drove a tractor for a farmer who wasn't a nice man at all. It made me determined I'd never be put in that position myself, and if I ever hired anybody else I'd make sure I did it better. But I think it made Giles just feel it wasn't worth trying, and he might as well have an easy life. Easy life!

'He started stealing when he was still at school. They threw him out, then he went to special school, still stealing. Then detention centres. Then prison. Every year he seemed to steal something bigger.'

Viola shyly pulled the picture of her dad from inside her locket.

'That's my dad,' she said quietly. 'He looks rather like you and your brother. He's done a bit of stealing too, and he's in prison now, for the raid on the Stanford bank three years ago. But he didn't do it. He admitted everything else, but he swears on his life he never did it.'

Sir Alex looked at the picture and turned his glance to PC Budakli. 'I lost touch with Giles around about then,' Sir Alex continued. 'He was always trying to get money out of me, and I helped him until he started trying to blackmail me – and that was the end. I did hear about this bank robbery and I couldn't help wondering if my brother had had anything to do with it, especially when I saw the photofit . . . But another man was found guilty . . . And what kind of man turns in his own brother?'

'But didn't you wonder if the gun in the cottage was anything to do with it?' I blurted out.

'No! Why would it occur to me? I hadn't thought about

that robbery since. Now I can see that Giles must have come back here to hide the gun, because it's where we spent so much time as kids. I wouldn't be surprised to find that there's a stash of money there somewhere, too . . .' Sir Alex glanced at PC Budakli, who was looking down at his enormous feet.

Mrs Armitage came over to look at the photo of Sir Alex's brother, then went back to her chair in silence, looking thoughtful.

In the ensuing embarrassed silence, Viola's little sister said, as she usually does: 'When's Daddy coming home?'

Sir Alex looked at PC Budakli. 'Soon, I'd say – wouldn't you?'

Sir Alex promised PC Budakli that he'd provide the police with any leads he could to find the missing Giles King. Then he shook hands with Viola, and then me and Callum.

'It can be a tough world, can't it?' he said to us. 'Giles has a wife and two young daughters of his own now, I believe. I've never met them.'

Viola shivered.

'So they're going to be in the exact same position as me and my mum and Bugsy,' she said.

'Yes,' said Sir Alex. 'But if he did do it, he has to take responsibility for it – which is something I'm afraid he's never done. And he has to take responsibility for what it will mean to them, too.'

'My Aunt Laura once said to me,' I began, 'that there are some bad people in the world, and a lot of them are somebody's father.'

'Your aunt's right. It's sad, but it's true. But maybe this is Giles's chance to stop being a bad person, though I won't hold my breath. And a chance for Viola's family to make a new start. Anything I can do to help with those things, I will.'

We all stood up, and said goodbye.

'Won't you stop for tea now we've got the hardest bit out of the way?' Sir Alex asked.

'They've got a show to finish, sir,' Callum said, in his best decisive Arlington Oratory voice.

'Ah yes, of course. Er . . . would it help if I came and introduced the second half? Wouldn't want to sweep that earlier . . . business . . . under the carpet, and it might help if I came and said it had all been a misunderstanding and everything was fine now.'

Miss Delaware looked as if she was going to explode with pinkness. 'That would be *wonderful!*' she squeaked. 'And wonder if we could possibly prevail on you to give a little summary of the story so far. People might have ended up a little confused after what happened.'

Sir Alex looked a bit pink himself at this. 'Not sure I'm . . . ah . . . the best person to do that,' he murmured.

Viola and I looked at each other, but avoided Miss Delaware's eye. He obviously hadn't the slightest clue what the story so far was in *The Maiden at the Mast* and who could blame him? After all, we hadn't either.

'They'll get back into it as we go along,' I said, giving Sir Alex a final parting handshake.

'The play's the thing,' he said.

'Right,' said Viola and Callum and I, all together.

Laura Hunt's Top Tips for Budding Writers:
Do not worry what your granny or mum would think. If you worry about whether your family will read your book and think badly of you, you will never write properly. You must feel free.

So the stake in the heart bit, and the maid dead of a broken neck is OK then.

A few weeks later, Viola and Callum and I were huddled up in the tree house. We were poring over the *Falmer Gazette*. The paper had the whole story of how Sir Alex's brother had finally been arrested, and had confessed to the Stanford bank robbery. It turned out that the gun was a replica. So he may not get such a long jail sentence.

'When you read it, it seems too amazing to be true,' said Viola. 'A millionaire with a wicked twin.'

'Yes,' I said. 'Aunt Laura told me that if she'd put it in one of her books her editor would have said it was all too unlikely. I said to her, "Truth is often stranger than fiction."'

The best thing was that Viola's dad had been released immediately, and was back home. There was a picture of the family all together on the front page, with Bugsy ceremonially tearing up her cardboard model of the prison cell. Viola looked like a different person these days, the smile never seemed to leave her face.

'It all turned out for the best, then,' I said, hopelessly trying to push Xerxes off the duvet.

'Depends on what you mean by "best",' Callum said, looking wise.

'Don't go all owly on us,' I told him. 'What do you mean?'

'Well, we're still stuck with the same unfair system, aren't we? Sir Alex is still stinky rich with servants and helicopters and stuff, and everybody else is still eating yesterday's chips and living in dustbins.'

He considered a cardboard carton lying on the floor.

'What's that?' Viola asked.

'Yesterday's Pot Noodles,' I said.

'There you are then,' Callum said triumphantly. 'Proof!'

'You're not living in a dustbin, you're living in a big house and going to a posh school you mizzling magsman,' I retorted, plumbing the depths of my Victorian insults yet again and throwing a well-aimed empty crisp packet at him.

'Sir Alex told my mum he'd give her money because of what happened with his brother,' Viola said. 'Apparently, he said he'd pay for me to go to a posh school too, if we wanted. My mum and dad said no thanks, they could manage.' Viola looked at me with that big sunny smile. 'I'm glad about that. I want to stay Falmer North.'

'You could have asked him for a nicer tree house,' I suggested. 'Maybe with a shower, microwave, wide-screen TV, perhaps one of those things that makes ice lollies.'

Callum was indignant.

'What's wrong with this one? It's been good enough for us all these years.'

We both threw crisp wrappers at him.

'EXACTICALLY!!' we both said at once.

There was a silence for a minute, except for Xerxes's purring. I rummaged under the duvet.

'Here's something else money can't buy,' I said. 'The Greatest Crime Novel Ever Writ, by the Greatest Crime Writer Ever to Live in a Tree House. Do you want to hear how *The Bat of the* D'*Urbervilles* ends?'

Viola giggled excitedly and looked at Callum, who was still pretending to be grumpy.

'Oh, go on then,' he finally said.

'Thanks for your enthusiastic support,' I said. 'Well, it goes like this . . .'

The Bat of the D'Urbervilles (ctd)

Having ascertained that Sir Horatio was unharmed, and leaving him in the tender care of the evil batman's beautiful brooding sister, who had fled the cottage in Horatio's wake when she realised what dark deeds her brother was pursuing, the dynamic duo followed the footprints through the mist. They led to a vast, dank cave overhung by rocky crags. The daring detectives crept forward only to fall back fearfully as a huge dark cloud erupted from the cave.

'Good God, Holmes. Bats! Thousands of them!'

Holmes and Watson ducked for safety as the never-ending stream of bats flew from their cave. After what seemed an age, the wild, mad fluttering ceased and a deadly silence fell.

They approached the cave and found a terrible sight. A huge mound of bat poo had buried the insane naturalist. Only the ears of his bat costume poked up from the ghastly foetid heap.

'We cannot save him, Watson. No man could survive that,' said Holmes.

'But I don't understand,' said Watson.

'Elementary, my dear Watson,' said Charlotte Holmes (which was a thing her brother Sherlock never actually said). 'The insane naturalist, who as I expect you now realise, had been sharpening his wicked arts on the ailing infants of Aylesbury, the demure damsels in Dunbar and the beastly burglary from the Barnstaple blood bank, had disguised himself as this fearsome vampire in order to play upon the superstitions of the local yokels and inherit the ancient seat of the D'Urbervilles, which he felt was, by right, his own. Seeing us emerging from the fog to catch him in our net of justice, he fled into this bat cave. But, alas for him, his fearful disguise was too good. The ordinary bats who live here were so spooked by what appeared to them to be a giant glowing version of one of their own relatives, that they all pooed furiously in terror – and so smothered him.'

'What a horrible fate, Holmes,' said Dr Callum Watson, his simple kindness showing through as he surveyed the two fake bat ears sinking with a squelch beneath the mountain of bat poo.

'He who lives by the bat shall die by the bat,' said Holmes, grimacing grimly.

The End

Laura Hunt's Top Tips for Budding Writers:
How do you end? You could try for a twist or unexpected ending, but, whatever you do, don't say 'I woke up and it was all a dream'.

Why not? That's more or less what Alice in Wonderland did. But a twist . . . hmmm. Dr Callum Watson as a vampire? Yes! Will now rewrite whole thing . . .

www.piccadillypress.co.uk

☆ The latest news on forthcoming books

☆ Chapter previews

☆ Author biographies

☆ Fun quizzes

☆ Reader reviews

☆ Competitions and fab prizes

☆ Book features and cool downloads

☆ And much, much more . . .

Log on and check it out!

Piccadilly Press